Dani pulled out her phone again and clicked on the news app. Streaming headlines spilled across the screen. Bank robbery in progress at Thunder City Bank & Trust.

She clicked on the headline. A coincidence. It had to be. There's no way it could be her branch.

The headline opened to a news feed. A reporter shouted into her microphone as T-CASS converged on the bank, her bank, right alongside the police. Gunshots could be heard in the background.

Nik. Dani forgot about her research at the thought of Nik phasing into all of that chaos. He'd already been shot once this year. Abilities or not, Alts could get hurt and they could die.

Dani ran out of the lab.

Cover Design by Deranged Doctor Design
Formatting by The Killion Group, Inc.
First Edition: January 12, 2016.

If you would like to know more about the Thunder City Series or about any of Debra Jess's other stories, you can subscribe to her newsletter or her Bookbub page at:
http://debrajess.com
Risk. Reward. Romance.
You can also follow her on any of these social media sites:
Facebook, Twitter, Tumblr, Pinterest, Bookbub, Instagram
If you want to be notified when Debra Jess's next novel is released, please sign up for her mailing list by going to http://www.debrajess.com

Your email address will never be shared and you can unsubscribe at any time.

A SECRET ROSE

A THUNDER CITY NOVELLA

DEBRA JESS

This story was written in memory of my grandmother, Rose. She danced like no one was watching, taught me how to bake rugeleh, and showed me how to win at seven card rummy.

CHAPTER ONE

Twenty years ago.

Eight-year-old Daniella Rose reached out and placed her hand on the large mirror over her dresser drawer. "I wish I may, I wish I might, have this wish I wish tonight."

Nothing happened. Dani hadn't vanished through the looking glass as Alice had done when she wished to visit Wonderland. No matter how hard she wished, she was still stuck in a dreary, dreadful world. Maybe tomorrow the words would work. The words must have worked for somebody or why would people say them?

Except she'd recited those same words every evening before dinner all winter. Dinner was the time of day when her parents aired their grievances about her — why did you get an A minus on that test, why didn't you braid your hair instead of letting it just hang there, why can't you sit still for more than two minutes — but it would be even worse now that Grandma Carmelita had moved in.

Grandma Carmelita had some very strange notions about girls. "Old fashioned," Dani had overheard one servant whisper to another.

Through the vents in the floor, she could hear her father arguing with Grandma Carmelita in the dining room. Something about hospitals, something about Robby. Robby was in the hospital again. Daniella would be going to the hospital tomorrow, too. Robby needed her liver or a piece of it, at least. Her father called it a transplant. Her Grandmother called it butchery.

"Doctors. Hospitals. You start putting the girl's body parts into the boy, and he will not be the same child. I tell you, this is madness. I have seen it for myself. Luca Fontane brought his child in for the same exact surgery. He came out a completely different child. Do you want your son to become like her? A vain, wicked creature? Always staring into mirrors, admiring herself? If only she were a boy."

Dani clenched her fists to keep from flying down the stairs and yelling at the old woman. It figured that her grandmother would think she was admiring herself. Heaven forbid she should compliment the granddaughter who'd done nothing but try to please her. She even wore the ugly, out-of-fashion dresses that her grandmother insisted she wear for dinner, for school, for church, for everywhere.

Dani squelched the tears before they flooded her eyes. Anger was better. Anger gave her power, even if it got her grounded more often than not. The fire in her belly raged hotter than it ever had before. Dani grabbed the flame and pulled it into her heart, keeping it there until it took hold. The fire burned until it hurt.

So, her Grandmother thought her vain and wicked? Fine. Vain and wicked the old woman would get.

Dani sat on the bed, her new plan more of a comfort than the bed itself. She could hear the crumple of paper under the mattresses where she'd shoved her most recent failure so she wouldn't have to see it. Stupid English teacher gave her an A minus. The Rose family didn't tolerate A minuses. Robby never got an A minus, but only because everyone felt sorry for him because he was so sick. He also got extra tutoring because he couldn't go to school. He got extra time to finish his assignments. It wasn't fair!

With a vicious tug, Dani yanked off one of the ugly patent-leather shoes her grandmother made her wear and tossed it at the useless mirror on her dresser. The shoe hit the mirror and knocked it off the wardrobe with a loud crash. *Very good*, the voice whispered in her ear. *Vain and wicked girls throw things. Vain and wicked girls are powerful. But, what would a boy do?*

Dani knew exactly what a boy would do. He would hit whoever was closest. Robby always hit her when no one was around to see. Dani tried to hit back once, but Robby ratted her out and she got her father's belt to her backside. How dare she hit her poor, sick brother?

The memory of leather on skin clenched her fist. Even to her eyes her hand looked small and useless. And, hitting the wall wouldn't hurt anyone but herself.

If only she could become a boy. Wouldn't that make her grandmother sorry? Vain, wicked, and a boy. Healthy, too. Her parents would hate her even more and it would be so delicious. Dani stripped off her dress.

"I wish I may, I wish I might, have this wish I wish tonight."

The gentle click in her brain took her by surprise. Fascinated, Dani watched as her skin stretched to accommodate her desire. It didn't hurt, but the odd sensation of spaghetti swirling in her stomach reminded her of the dinner she wasn't allowed to eat because of the A minus. It took less than a minute, but when when her skin stopped stretching, the swirling sensation also stopped, and Dani smiled.

Maybe there was something to the prayers her grandmother insisted she recite. God had made her a boy.

Joy washed through her. For a moment, she forgot about the vain, wicked child she'd sworn she'd become and raced to get redressed, this time in her jumper, which was big enough to cover her now-larger body. Finally, her parents would be satisfied with her. Maybe her grandmother would be happy to spend time with her.

As her hand touched the door knob, her eyes stopped on her fourth-grade class picture tacked up on her wall. Nikolaos Blackwood stood behind her. She'd cut everyone else out of the picture except herself and Nik. His hand rested on her shoulder, and Dani remembered the joy of knowing he was right behind her, his eyes the color of Mystic Bay, his smile as bright as the sun reflecting water. Everyone liked Nik, the boy who could disappear into the walls and travel underground without even trying. Everyone called him "Ghost" because his voice sounded like a ghost when he talked from the walls. He was an Alt and all the girls loved him, including Dani.

Dani looked down at her body again. Would Nik like her if she were a boy? She knew some boys liked other boys the way that girls liked boys, but she didn't think Nik did. He was a year older because she had skipped a grade. He knew more about boys liking girls than she did.

The lump in her throat choked her. What did she

want more? Her grandmother's approval? Her family's love? Or Nik?

She looked at the picture as more shouting rose from the vent. Reality sucked her hopes for a peaceful family down into the dusty vent. All her parents wanted from her were her body parts to give to Robby. Nik might love her if she tried hard enough, though. If she stayed a girl.

Dani turned away from the door and took off her jumper, hanging it back in the closet so she wouldn't get into trouble again. With the jumper no longer restricting her movements, Dani prayed again. "Please make me a girl."

The changed happened even faster this time. Dani put on her pajamas, the vain, wicked girl subdued for the moment. The argument downstairs still raged. Dani crawled into bed. She closed her eyes and imagined Nik. Would he think that not telling anyone about the boy side of her was lying? Nik never lied.

Nik doesn't have to lie, the vain, wicked girl whispered. *His parents love him. He can disappear. He can travel fast. You're just Robby's little sister. Becoming a boy won't change that.*

For Nik, she'd remain a girl.

CHAPTER TWO

Three days after the events in Blood Surfer.

Nik waited until he'd cleared company security before side-stepping into the nearest wall of Generation Med. His errand wasn't a happy one, but the thought of seeing Daniella Rose again sparked a smile. He'd lost track of her after high school, but it hadn't taken a lot of investigating to find her. Luckily for him, Dani had only moved back from Star Haven to Thunder City this week. As an Alt, and a rather prominent one, he wasn't allowed to cross Mystic Bay to Star Haven. Or rather, he could, but he risked arrest and imprisonment. The quarry raid three days ago had left Star Haven leaderless and confused. A few brave souls had stepped forward to act in the capacity of an interim government, but their focus was on public protection and the enforcement of the law — and that included the hated Alt ban. Nik would have risked crossing the Bay for Dani, though. The message he had to deliver needed to be done in person. A letter just wouldn't be proper.

Proper? Who are you kidding? You're curious. You didn't do right by her back in high school. You should have done

*more to stop the other kids from bullying her, but you didn't.
You were too busy with your own circle of friends. You were
no hero to Daniella Rose. You want to see if she's managed to
shed her bad-girl reputation on her own.*

Nik grimaced at the thought as he slipped along
the walls to the second floor, end of the hallway, first
door on the left. Sure he was curious. If you had asked
anyone at Kensington Academy where Daniella would
have wound up ten years after graduation, most would
have said she'd be in the city jail. They had, in fact,
been right. Thankfully, she hadn't stayed in jail for long.

He unphased through the doors and paused, taking
in the layout of the lab. Fresh paint mixed with damp
cardboard puckered his nose, and the hum of electricity
in the fluorescent lighting interrupted the silence. The
light *tap-tap* of fingers on a keyboard echoed from
behind a stack of half-unpacked equipment. More
boxes lay in neat rows along work tables.

Nik phased into the boxes so as not to alert whoever
sat behind them. From there he sank into the floor,
under a single desk chair, and up the back wall.

From his vantage point in the wall he could see
Dani sitting at the single computer console, her long,
painted nails typing without hesitation, her lower lip
tucked adorably into her mouth, and her pencil skirt
revealing legs that would make a man tumble to the
floor and beg for mercy. Thank God, he couldn't fall
anywhere while phased. He also couldn't unphase
until he got himself back under control. What the
hell had happened? Despite her reputation, or maybe
because of it, Dani's magnetic sexiness had left a trail
of adolescent broken hearts behind her at Kensington,
but Nik's hadn't been one of them.

Oh, really?

No, really. He'd had the perfect girlfriend back then — or, so he had thought.

Dani leaned back in her chair with a yawn and a stretch. Unintended law of motion: the harder Dani stretched the higher her breasts rose, the buttons on her blouse doing little to cover her cleavage. Shit, he was in trouble. Without warning, she stopped in mid-stretch, her brows crumpling before she jumped out of her chair, hands on slim hips.

"Why, Nikolaos Blackwood, as I live and breathe. What are you doing hiding in the walls of my laboratory?"

In his phased state, the solid matter he merged with vibrated ever so slightly as he "breathed". Most people wouldn't notice it if he kept to one small corner of the room, but if he spread himself out across an entire wall, then someone who knew what to look for — like Dani — could tell he was there.

No point in staying phased any longer. He stepped out of the wall to Dani's left, walking through her work station until he stood right next to her. "You caught me."

"I couldn't miss all your heavy breathing. Enjoy the view?" She tugged at the top button of her blouse.

Nik rolled his eyes. "How could I not, short stuff?" At five foot nothing, even in stilettos, pretty much every guy after eighth grade who talked to Dani got a nice view.

Dani punched his arm. "C'mere then, and give me a hug."

He did, pulling her off the ground just because he could.

She laughed, a sweet song. "Okay. Okay. Consider your machismo duly noted, showoff. Now, put me down. Slowly. I don't want to break a heel."

He did, slowly, her body rubbing against his. For heaven's sake, how was he supposed to deliver his message when all he wanted to do was sweep Dani off her feet again? Hold her close again.

"Let's take a look at you." Dani stepped back with elevator eyes, all snap and humor and the most delicate shade of lavender he'd seen nowhere else. How could he have forgotten the color of her eyes? "You're not in uniform, so you're not here to seduce me away from the private sector into city government. You're not in one of those three-piece suits you favor for visiting clients, but you're still wearing midnight blue, so you must be here to talk about something serious."

How did she know he favored three-piece suits for his other job? Did his father favor three-piece suits? Did the other male investigators for his father's private investigation firm wear them? Nik tried to remember what everyone had worn yesterday at their monthly meeting. Faces he knew as well as his own blended together with what they wore. He'd have to pay closer attention next time he was in the office.

To cover his confusion, Nik reached down to take Dani's tiny hands in his. "You're right. There is something I need to discuss with you."

Dani squeezed his hands, her brows lowered with genuine concern. "Perhaps we shouldn't talk here. It's too distracting, too confining. Let's head out for lunch."

Nik's heart relaxed. "I could go for some lunch. What do you have in mind?"

Dani flipped her long brown hair over one shoulder and plucked a sweater off the back of her chair. "Around this neighborhood, there isn't much. Why don't we stop at the grocer's on the corner? Since the company hasn't opened its cafeteria yet and I'm the only one here today, I can be a little flexible with my lunch hour. How about a picnic at West Ridge Park?"

The park was closer to the harbor, but at least a half hour hike from Generation Med headquarters. Too long a drive by car or public transportation. Luckily, he had an alternative.

"C'mere." He held out his arms.

Dani's gorgeous eyes opened wide. "Wait, are you sure?"

Nik had never been more sure in his life. "It won't hurt. I promise."

Dani stepped into his personal space, maybe a little closer than necessary.

"What about security?" she asked. Nik understood. In a cutting-edge start-up like Generation Med, you didn't enter or leave the building without a search.

"We'll stop by security first. Grocer's second, then the park." Nik wrapped his arms around her waist, also not necessary. "Don't hold your breath. Breathe normally. If you want to, you can close your eyes."

Dani looked up at him, all spitfire. "Oh, honey. I never close my eyes."

Nik held her gaze before he slipped them both into the floor.

~★~

The last person Dani expected to waltz into her lab was Nik Blackwood. Damn. Even after ten years, he could still make her heart pound like a punching bag before a prize fight. Of course, she had never told Nik about her feelings for him. Not in elementary school. Not in middle school. Certainly not at Kensington. Trouble had followed her throughout those years no matter how fast she ran to escape it. Despite the rumors — always behind her back, but she had ways of finding out — she'd never dated any of those silly boys in high school. Not even Nik, not that he had asked. He wouldn't have. Dani's life had too much drama for steady-as-a-rock, goody-two-shoes, Nik Blackwood. His romance with Serena Jakes, also known as Highlight, was the type of romance all young girls lived for.

Yet he had never married her, though they had been engaged several times over the past decade, if the online gossip columns were to be believed. Even as recently as this week, rumor had it that Ghost and Highlight were back together. Dani assumed they'd hooked-up after the quarry raid. Nothing like the surge of adrenaline to reignite your love, or lust, or whatever they had.

"Here we are," Nik announced as he popped both of them out above ground.

Dani looked down at herself. "Well, look at that. Not a spec of dirt on me despite traveling through mud, concrete, metals and God knows what else underground. Even our bag of food is clean. How on earth do you do that?"

Nik guided her over to a picnic table. "Simple. If we're not solid until we're out of the ground, there's nothing for the dirt to cling to."

Dani sat opposite Nik, her hand already reaching for the napkins. "Did you ever bother with a driver's license or do you just phase to wherever you want to go?"

Nik laughed, but with a twinge of sadness. Whatever he was going to tell her — and Dani had a few thoughts as to what it might be — it would no doubt hurt. Dani steeled herself while she opened a container of macaroni salad.

"I have a license," he said, but didn't elaborate.

Oooooh, this wasn't good.

Dani munched on her salad and waited for Nik to say something, while he took his time eating his sandwich.

"I saw your brother two days ago," he said finally, putting down half his sandwich.

"Do you mean he made an appointment to hire you to find me, or did he just accost you on the street?" The bitterness hadn't dulled in ten years. Dani had tried to kick the vain, wicked girl she had been to the curb before she moved to Star Haven, but every once in a while the evil side of her crawled off the curb to bring the oncoming traffic of Dani's life to a screeching halt.

Nik winced. "A little of both, I guess. He approached me outside the courthouse and asked to take me to lunch."

Robby? Politely asking an Alt to do lunch? Nik wouldn't look at her. No, Robby had accosted him, probably demanded Nik talk to him, and threatened to embarrass Nik until he agreed. Robby understood the social niceties, but didn't believe such rules applied to him. He always got what he wanted and if he didn't, his parents — their parents — would make it happen.

"Let me guess. Robby needs another transplant. Which body part this time?" He already had part of her liver, pancreas, and intestines. By rights she shouldn't have donated anything to him. The medical community determined years ago that transplants from alternative humans could have unintended consequences. Since no one knew how Alts generated their abilities, no doctor wanted to risk giving a normal human Alt powers or risk interrupting Alt powers in the alternative human. She hadn't known that when she was a child, and since she had never told anyone, not even her parents, of her Alt ability, the transplants continued without obvious consequences.

"He needs a kidney." Nik fussed with his sandwich instead of looking at her. "He would have asked you himself except he didn't know where to find you, and time is running short."

"Nonsense." Dani put down her container. "He doesn't dare ask me himself because I threatened to refuse any more transplants until he learned to treat me with respect. Robby respects no one but himself and he knows that everyone hates him. He's afraid I'll say no and he'll be stuck with a random kidney plucked from the donor list. Robby would never settle for a substandard body part."

The story was true, for the most part. She had threatened to put a stop to any more transplants until Robby smartened up. Oh, how he'd turned bright red with repressed outrage, but he knew she could and she would refuse. Her parents on the other hand, she'd threatened a different way: from the Thunder City jail when they had refused to bail her out. Their haughty tones over the tinny phone line brought out the vain, wicked girl like no one else had before. She'd reminded them that while Robby was healthy at the moment, she would turn eighteen in less than a month. After that, she could and would cheerfully refuse any more transplants.

Her parent's lawyer, one of the best in the city, arrived within the hour and had the case against her thrown out.

Vain and wicked won the day back then, but earning back her soul took a long time. She wouldn't refuse Robby now, no matter the temptation.

Nik knew none of this of course. He felt sorry for Robby, as most people did. Nik would never turn away a person in need, no matter how rude they were.

Nik was a saint and she was the sinner. They ought to mix like oil and water, but Dani didn't care. Giving up the possibility of tenure at Star Haven University and returning to Thunder City rubbed her raw in all of the wrong places. Damned Alt ban. She'd been careful about where and when she'd shifted into her male half — Daniel — for years, but she couldn't hide that part of herself forever. Not if she wanted a relationship. Not if she wanted someone special.

Not if she wanted Nik.

"So will you do it?"

"What? Give him my kidney?" Dani realized her concentration had drifted into dangerous territory. Love, relationships. Not something she wanted to think about right now. She picked up her container and scooped out more macaroni. "Why yes, of course, I will."

Nik gave her a doubtful look.

"Oh, don't look at me like that, Nik. I've changed. I know it's hard to believe, but I've reformed my wild ways — mostly." She gave him a saucy wink for good measure.

Nik laughed a little. "Are you sure? I remember your wild ways. I also remember that you and Robby never got along. I'm not here to pressure you or bribe you. Regardless of your decision, I still want to take you out for dinner."

Score one for the good girl. Old vain and wicked could suck it. "Nik Blackwood, I do think you overestimate your charm. Regardless of whether or not you take me out for dinner *and* dancing, I will still give my good-for-nothing brother a kidney. I'll do it because it's the right thing to do. Believe it or not, I'm really a nice person once you get to know me."

Nik pushed aside the garbage from their lunch to grab her hands again. Startled Dani leaned into the challenge radiating from Nik's eyes. "Nice, huh. All right, Daniella Rose. Dinner and dancing tonight, and we'll see just how nice you are."

Dani's toes curled in her shoes. It would seem mild mannered Nik Blackwood had a wilder side than she had expected. "You're on. My place. Seven p.m. Don't be late."

~★~

Nik popped out of the ground in front of Dani's doorstep right on time, a bouquet of mixed pastel-colored blooms in his hand. He had debated with himself over whether the flowers were overkill, then decided not to overthink the date. His last date four nights ago, with Serena, had ended the way their relationship always ended: badly. She'd insisted he hadn't thought enough about where they were going, what they'd do when they got there, and how their date would impact their T-CASS duties.

After ten years together and three broken engagements, Nik realized he'd had enough of the over-structured life Serena demanded of him. He'd had enough of dating someone who reminded him of his mother.

The front door to Dani's tiny cape house flew open just as he raised his hand to knock. And just like that, Nik knew he'd made the right decision.

"Flowers!" she squealed with all the thrill of a ten-year-old ripping open a wrapped birthday gift. She stepped outside and yanked the bouquet out of his hands, inhaling the scent, long and deep. Nik tried to keep his eyes on her face, but her shimmery blouse didn't hide as much as he wished it would.

"How did you know I loved flowers?" she asked. "Come inside. I want to get these into water right away."

Nik caught the screen door before it slammed closed so that he would walk through the doorway like a Norm instead of through the closed door. Dani didn't notice; the *click-click* of her way-too-high heels led him down a short hallway to the kitchen. His investigator's eye took in the soft colors of the home's interior, interrupted by a few paintings on the walls. The furniture complimented the colors, but looked older, as if she'd bought it used. The style fit Dani, but it didn't mesh with the girl who had grown up in one of the wealthiest neighborhoods in Thunder City, not far from where Nik and his brothers had lived.

"Here, let me." Nik stretched to grab a small vase from the top shelf of a cabinet.

"Show off," Dani said, with a nudge of her elbow to his stomach. Her smile, though, told him she appreciated his assistance. "There we go. A little water and I'll set them right here in the center of the dining table. They'll be the first thing I see when I come down for breakfast in the morning."

Nik leaned on the nearest wall, appreciating Dani rather than flowers. A subtle click caught his attention. Fearing he'd broken something, he leaned away, but at first he didn't see what had shifted under his arm. It took a second in the low light, but then he saw the outline of a panel embedded in the wall. He touched the panel with this fingertips in the right spot. The panel slid open to reveal a screen.

Dani noticed his examination. "Security," she said as she fussed with the flowers. "The Fargrounds is an okay neighborhood, but for a single gal like me, a little extra protection isn't a bad thing."

"Of course." Nik slid the panel closed again. He agreed on principle, but he recognized the system. His stepfather, Thomas Carraro, designed security systems for government buildings, multi-national corporations, and the occasional residential home in wealthy neighborhoods like the one where he and Dani had lived as children. This system went far and above what a "single gal" like Dani would need in a home like this. In fact, the system would have cost more than the house.

Why would Dani need such an overabundance of security? Why did she live here in the Fairgrounds in the first place? Even if her parents had cut her off, she must make a better than average salary at Generation Med.

A fierce need to protect Dani swept over him. He pulled her into a hug.

"What's this all about?" She looked up at him, her lavender eyes large and questioning.

"I just wanted a hug from the prettiest girl in Thunder City," Nik said, to cover all the questions he knew he shouldn't ask. Not tonight, at least.

"Well then." Dani stood up on tip-toe, as far as her heels allowed, and puckered her lips.

Nik laughed, all those questions pushed to the far back of his brain. If Dani wanted a kiss he'd have to lean down to give one to her. A quick smack on the lips. It wasn't enough, not nearly enough. His lips ached for a more thorough kiss, but it was too soon.

"I usually don't allow boys to kiss me on the first date." She pulled out of his arms, her hands guiding him back down the hallway toward the door. "And, certainly not before they buy me dinner, but for you, Nik Blackwood, I'll make an exception."

He'd make an exception, too. Instead of shutting off his brain so he could enjoy the evening, leaving the care of Thunder City to his fellow T-CASS colleagues, he'd keep his investigator eyes open. Even while Dani locked the front door, Nik scanned her postage-stamp front yard for lurking shadows.

You don't invest in the type of security system Dani had without serious consideration. Is that why Dani lived in the Fargrounds? Because she needed the security more than she needed a larger home?

"Looking for your fans?" Dani turned to him, hands on hips.

Nik finished his sweep of their location. Nothing out of the ordinary, but he knew better than most that true villains never left traces you could see in plain sight. "No. Just making sure the paparazzi didn't follow me here."

"I don't see how they could." Dani stepped into his personal space again, her arms slipping around his waist, her head tilted back, her lips begging for another kiss. "Following you would be like playing whack-a-mole. You raise your head above ground and whack!" She smacked his backside. "You disappear again."

"Ouch! That hurt." No joke. Dani looked all sweet and delicate, but she had hidden power in her swing.

"Awww, poor Nik. No more stalling. I'm hungry."

Dani had always been aggressive, defending herself against the subtle or not so subtle threats leveled at her during school hours. As a classmate, Nik had assumed that she was fearless, strong, determined. Through the filter of adulthood, he now wondered if she'd been afraid instead. Students always knew how to get at each other, even under the watchful eyes of Kensington's instructors. Dani had always come out on top.

Could Dani be scared now? Had she purchased Thomas's system because of a specific threat? In the Fargrounds, it was unlikely she would run into anyone from her past.

Nik took one last, discreet look over her shoulder at her neighbor's yard. Nothing to see there, and he didn't want to upset her by looking over his shoulder at the other yard behind him. He pulled her into an embrace, the sense of protectiveness becoming more powerful the longer he held her close.

Scared or brave, determined or playful, no one was going to hurt Dani. Nik sank her into the ground where he ruled as king of his own domain. No one could follow her where he would take her. He would do what he had to, fight any battle, to keep her safe.

CHAPTER THREE

The manic up-tempo bass line pounded a rhythm under the multi-colored lights on the dance floor. Dani swung her hips in time to the music, her feet matching each beat while she swung her arms in the air with graceful abandon. Not since she'd left Star Haven had she felt so at home — maybe too much at home. Nik wasn't stupid. He remembered her wilder days. He remembered her arrest. Her case had been dismissed, but newspapers never forgot.

Nik watched her from the sidelines, having bowed out during the last song, claiming self-defense. Even as another dancer sidled up to her, Dani kept her eyes on Nik as she gyrated. Just him. His predatory gaze was so possessive and so unlike what she expected from goody-two-shoes Nik. No one had ever looked at her like that. Not even. . . .

With a vicious kick of her heels to dispel the memory, Dani almost hit the poor guy dancing in front of her. He stumbled out of the way just in time and managed not to knock anyone else over. To make up for her faux pas, Dani playfully pulled him back into her circle, careful to keep as polite a distance as possible on the crowded floor. When the song ended, the guy leaned close to her ear with a sexy suggestion. Dani laughed.

Maybe in another lifetime she'd have taken him up on his offer. Tonight, though, she thanked him kindly, kissed the tip of her forefinger, tapped the guy's nose, then skipped off the dance floor.

"What was that all about?" Nik handed her a drink. Just what she needed to soothe her dry throat.

"I almost kicked the guy in the shins," she replied between sips. "I gave him a quick apology."

Nik put down his own drink, his eyes on the dance floor. "Is he going to be trouble?"

The next song started, but the guy stood there watching the two of them. He wasn't approaching them, but he wasn't dancing either. A sexy fellow like that probably wasn't used to a woman rejecting him. Dani sighed, regretting that she'd gotten so lost in the music. She'd forgotten how stupid men could be, especially after a few drinks.

"Nothing I can't handle." Even wearing her killer heels, she still had to tilt her head all the way back to talk to him. Good, he'd turned his attention to her and away from the other guy. Nik stroked the waves of hair tumbling down her back, but then turned his head back to the guy on the dance floor — who by now had gathered his courage and decided to confront Nik.

Her flirty nature was about to start a bar fight. Music walloped her ear-drums, and she could feel the tension rolling off of Nik.

Stop this. Stop it now, the good girl in her whispered.

Oh, come on. When was the last time a guy started a bar fight in your honor, the vain, wicked girl whispered back.

Her blood boiled, reveling in the idea of two men fighting over her. Vain and wicked almost won out, until Nik slipped off his stool and rolled up his sleeves, ready to throw a punch.

You're going to lose him. He'll blame you for instigating this and you'll lose him. Good guys like Nik don't start bar fights.

Good girl won the battle. It was time to cut and run.

"Let's get out of here." She reached for Nik's hand.

Nik stopped before he took a step, his blue eyes back on her where they belonged, repressed rage caught short but begging to be released.

"Nik, really, it was just an apology. I wasn't thinking. I almost took his knee cap off with these things." She swung her stiletto up to demonstrate. "Don't start anything here. Not tonight. Please."

In a flash, he wrapped an arm around her waist to pull her close. Just like the guy on the dance floor, he leaned toward her ear, but instead of whispering something delicious, he sucked her earlobe, dangling earring and all, between his teeth.

"Oh!" Her eyes widened as Nik's tongue massaged the sensitive flesh until her knees turned weak. She had to push him away before she fell to the floor. "I'll repeat myself. Pay the tab and get me out of here."

Get me out before vain and wicked returns.

~★~

Nik unphased her into the middle of a room she didn't recognize. Judging by the moody, monochrome colors, the paintings of wildlife, and the latest gadgets in entertainment occupying one corner, she guessed Nik had brought her to his place. Her heels settled into a thick carpet, keeping her a touch off balance.

Nik's arms tightened around her. Oh, so Nik wanted her balance under his control? Well, that was a problem because if her adrenaline didn't find an outlet soon, she'd have to wrestle her control back from Nik. Wrestling with Nik — what a lovely thought.

"You'll have to tell me someday how you manage to find your way around the city while underground," she said, her voice husky. "And, so quickly."

His laugh sounded more like a purr, rubbing her desire just long enough to tease. "I travel by instinct."

"I see. What is your instinct telling you now? Do you do everything just as quickly?"

His hand skimmed up the back of her dress and tugged the catch. Her dress fell to the edge of her shoulders. "You don't want to see how quick I can be. Some things need to be taken slowly."

She shivered as Nik's fingers glided down her naked back. Oh, yes, everything they did tonight should be taken slowly.

"Can I get you a drink?" he whispered in her ear.

His warm breath made her wish he'd taste her again.

"What do you have?" She couldn't hold back the quiet moan.

"There's a bottle of 1945 Saint Julien I've been saving for a special occasion."

Dani jerked her head back and not because of the wine he'd selected. "You consider me a special occasion?"

"I consider you special."

Dani stilled. Even for her, the emotion behind Nik's words caressed her in places she'd locked away a long time ago. A special one-night stand, she expected, but from Nik's lips it sounded as if he expected more. Before she could comment, Nik stepped away, heading into the next room. His absence created a cool space where he'd stood in front of her. Well, if Nik wanted special, she'd give him special. With practiced moves, she stepped out of her shoes and slipped off her dress.

Nik returned and stopped dead in the doorway.

"Like what you see?" She did a quick spin to show off her lacy black underwear.

Before she finished the spin Nik stood in front of her, the wine bottle dangling loose by his side.

"Why don't you let me take that before you drop it and break your toe." With a tug, she pulled the wine bottle away from him, catching the cork remover with nimble fingers. Nik still looked down at her, his blue eyes narrow under heavy lids. She stepped closer, her wrist twisting the cork remover into place with practiced ease. A moment later, the she popped open the bottle. "You forgot the glasses."

"We won't need any glasses."

Before Dani could protest, Nik swept her up into his arms. "Careful, darling. I don't want to waste a drop of this..." she checked the wine's label, "...Chateau Beychevelle Magnum."

She laid her head on Nik's shoulder as he walked her into another room. His bedroom, where he lowered her onto his bed as if she would shatter. What Nik needed to learn was that it would take a lot more than dropping her onto a firm mattress to make her shatter, but there was also the wine bottle to consider. Before he could go any further, Dani placed the tip of the bottle against her lips and sucked in the potent liquid. From the corner of her eye, she could see Nik watching her with a thirsty look. She imagined he wanted to snatch the bottle away so he could devour her himself. She had better plans.

Taking one last mouthful she held it in her mouth as she set the bottle on the nightstand. She wrapped her hand around Nik's nape and pulled him in for a wine-drenched kiss. The rough shadow on his chin scraped her taste buds, the friction exciting her more than the wine.

"Oh, honey, I've waited so long for this. You taste so good."

"What do I taste like?" His whisper sent shivers cascading from her hair down to her toes.

"Sugar cookies and caramel and maple syrup. All of the sweet stuff mixed into one delicious package."

He groaned as her tongue continued its trail down his neck. For a moment he squirmed away from her, just long enough to remove his shirt and pants. Then he joined her on the bed, his body pressed against hers, all planes and angles and firm muscle. No scars, either. Considering he'd been shot in the chest the week before, she'd expected to see at least a bruise where the bullet had hit. She'd have to ask him about that later. Tonight, his body was her playground.

"If you want me to stop, tell me now," she whispered.

"No. Don't stop. Just give me one moment."

She waited while he reached inside the drawer of the night stand. Nik, the Boy Scout, was always prepared. The second he finished, she rolled him onto his back, her smaller body just the right size to mold herself against his stomach while she teased one of his nipples with her tongue, and her hand slipped through the fine hair of his chest to rub the other one.

"Do you like that?"

Instead of answering, he slipped one hand under her bra strap and loosened it. She straddled his torso to sit up far enough to slide out of the bra. Then she lay back down on him so she could wiggle out of her underwear. He groaned as the friction she'd created increased.

Every inch of her connected with his skin. Physically, he was ready for her, but a small voice inside her head needed confirmation.

"Are you sure you want to finish this?"

Once again, he didn't respond. Instead, he reared up and wrapped his arms about her waist before twisting her around so he could roll on top of her. Who would have thought Nik liked it rough? Fine with her. She could bottom like a good girl when she chose to.

The second she surrendered herself, the sense of safety overwhelmed her. Safe in Nik's arms was more beautiful than she could have imagined. She had no cares or worries as he massaged her muscles, working his way down her body to the point where her pleasure started.

She giggled as he pulled her inside his mouth, the full force of the wine warming her blood. She arched up while Nik worked his way back up to her breasts. No fair teasing her like that. She tugged his hair.

"You're killing me, Blackwood. Kiss me. Kiss me now and get yourself inside me before I toss you on your back again."

He laughed his disbelief that she could force him off her and onto his back. Best for now to let him think she couldn't. Most men preferred to orchestrate their pleasure, and while she wouldn't dream of describing Nik as "most men", she didn't want to interrupt his extended, oh-so-erotic moan as he slid inside her.

She rocked against him as hard as she could, matching his rhythm, holding off the final climax until she couldn't stand it anymore. A final thrust brought her closer to euphoria than she'd ever experienced with anyone else. Was it because this was Nik? Her feelings while her body sang said yes, only Nik could make her feel this euphoric. Nik slowed down, his own body satisfied, his skin sensitive to her touch.

From beneath him, Dani wrapped her arms around his shoulders and pulled him down on top of her.

"Wait, I'm too heavy."

"Not for me, Nik. You're not too heavy for me."

He obliged. She tucked in her chin at the juncture of his neck and jaw, and purred just loud enough for him to hear her while she rubbed her nose along his cheek.

"Are you trying to kill me?"

"Oh, honey, I'm just getting warmed up. Don't tell me you're done for the night."

He muttered something rude, but she didn't hear another complaint. She continued to tempt him until she took control once more. Twenty minutes later they both climaxed, this time with Dani on top.

With Nik still inside her, she stretched. "What time is it?"

Nik harumphed something below her. This time they'd tangled the sheets and the comforter was balled up in the corner of the bed, blocking her view of the clock.

"Gotta move, babe. I can't check the time from here." She lifted herself off of him. As she reached over to push the blankets out of the way, Nik slid a hand up her torso to caress her breast. Surprising. "You want to do this again?"

"Do you?" He sounded hopeful.

She checked the time. "Sorry, stud, but it's almost two a.m. and I have to go to work tomorrow."

He muttered something equally rude about her employers. Oh, Nik was going to be a handful, but she loved men who couldn't get enough of her. At least until they learned her secret, which would happen sooner rather than later if she fell asleep here. More often than not, she shifted in her sleep, which was not how she planned to let Nik meet Daniel. She playfully slapped his hand away.

"Hate to break up the party, but I have boxes to unpack, reports to write, and manifests to complete."

He sat up and pulled her into a hug. His kiss came as an unexpected bonus for the night. Not a kiss to ignite more rolling around in the sheets, but a kiss of true affection.

"What was that for?"

"Everything. Nothing. Just for you."

Shit. Nik unlocked her heart. She was in trouble and she knew it. Which made her decision to leave his bed that much easier.

She couldn't see his face in the dark, which meant he also couldn't see hers, either. "Nik. Tonight meant a lot to me. My job though, it means a lot to me, too. I can't put it at risk. Not even for you, not for more of. . . ." She couldn't finish the sentence, but she didn't have to.

"I'm sorry," he said. "Of course. You need to work and so do I. I have a long day tomorrow chasing down Fredek Varga."

A cold wave of recognition frosted over all of Dani's warm spots. She hoped her voice didn't shake. "Fredek Varga? You mean Fagin, the drug lord?"

"Yeah, that's him." Nik rolled away, reaching for his pants. "You remember him?"

"I thought he was in jail for at least another thirteen years." Dani reached for the wine bottle. Examining the bottle hid her face while Nik got dressed. Fagin was free. Any doubts she had about purchasing that expensive Carraro security system melted away.

"Changing drug laws. He's completed a few rehab programs and he's been a model prisoner the entire time. The city jail needs room. Mom thinks the quarry raid might give more Star Haven residents an excuse to move to Thunder City. A few of the more violent anti-Alt organizations might take advantage of the population shift to send some of their people over here to cause trouble. We need to be ready."

Mom. He meant Catherine Blackwood, Captain Spectacular, CEO of Blackwood Enterprises and leader of Thunder City's Alt Support Services — Nik's other job when he wasn't working as a private investigator. The Rose family had often attended city functions with the Blackwoods. She knew about Dani's arrest. God knew what she would do if she found out Dani was sleeping with her son.

"Nik, a guy like Fagin can't be rehabbed. He's going to rebuild his blitz distribution network all over again. Thunder City will become what the Swamp in Star Haven is right now — a cesspool of blitz addicts and their suppliers. It'll be the drug wars all over again." She would know that better than most, better than Nik, better than all of the combined strategists of T-CASS.

Nik leaned across the bed. He cradled the back of her head with one large hand and pulled her close for an intimate kiss that made her briefly consider staying a while longer. "I know. Which is why I'm going to keep an eye on him. Not officially, but if I just happen to see something suspicious while off duty, I can at least let T-CASS know. They'll keep a record until we have official confirmation that he's back in business."

It sounded good, but T-CASS operated within the law. It was their mission to work with Thunder City's police, not as vigilantes. A guy like Fagin had manipulated the system for over a decade. He knew how to hide himself behind the law. At least he did until his right-hand man betrayed him. The Artful

Dodger. Dani, back when she was a vain and wicked young man.

"Don't go anywhere," she ordered with a playful slap to Nik's backside.

She collected her clothes from the other room and took a few minutes to wash up before redressing. The bathroom alone was almost the size of her kitchen. Nik lived well, but she'd expected that. An Alt and a Blackwood had to live someplace secure, even in an Alt-friendly community like Thunder City.

When she stepped back out she discovered Nik had flipped on the bedroom lights and had changed into his Ghost uniform. According to what she'd read in the papers, the form-fitting black outfit was made of some sort of super-secret composite material designed especially for members of T-CASS.

"I'll take you home."

"You don't have to. I can take a taxi." She had work to do and none of it related to Generation Med.

"Dani." He crossed the room and took her hands into his. "I'm escorting you home."

The authority in his voice brooked no argument. Any other day, the take-charge attitude would have charmed her. Tonight, she had to tolerate it for the sake of keeping her secret a secret. She had no good reason to deny him. For tonight, she'll be the compliant lady who did as her man asked.

"As you wish," she said with a well-practiced fake laugh, holding out her arms. He pulled her closer to him, closer than necessary, and phased her into the wall.

CHAPTER FOUR

Nik didn't bother with the front door this time. He phased Dani directly into her kitchen, his senses alert for anything out of place. He didn't want to leave her behind. He wouldn't leave her alone in her own house until he was sure it was safe.

The kitchen was quiet and still except for the low tick of a clock. He heard nothing from the rest of the house. The powerful protective feeling remained, even as he chided himself for letting his imagination get the best of him.

He safeguarded people for a living. You couldn't belong to T-CASS without possessing the willingness to die in the service of saving others. Yet his work for T-CASS never overrode his sense of order, of responsibility. He always approached each job with a clear head and a plan of action, whether it was a fire engulfing a high rise, a multi-car accident on the highway, or a home invasion gone very wrong.

So why did all of his training abandon him when he was with Dani? None of his T-CASS teammates needed his specific talents for protection either. Their training program drilled teamwork into them. Serena would have scowled at him and followed up with a lecture if he'd insisted on escorting her home, no matter how romantic the evening might have been.

"I don't see any boogie men, do you?" Dani untangled herself from his arms.

Nik sighed, reluctant to admit he had no excuse to stay any longer. "No. No boogie men."

She kissed him, not with passion but with finality mixed with a touch of humor. It was time for him to leave.

He loved her humor. Even more than that, he loved when she laughed with him, her voice giving him the chills even as it loosened his stress. He watched her walk away from him, out of the kitchen and down the hallway, trusting him to let himself out.

He loved the way she moved, her hair all wild and swinging down her back. He loved the way she focused on him, just him, when he talked, instead of multitasking with her phone. She acted as if he were the most important person in the world to her. He loved. . . .

No, it was too soon for that. His lust was getting the better of him.

This second visit also gave him another chance for a discreet examination of her security system. This time he knew what subtle signs to look for, hidden triggers no one would have noticed without a trained eye. His first assessment had been correct. This system had been designed by Thomas Carraro, one of his custom jobs. Nik would bet his next paycheck on it.

Dani turned on the shower upstairs. It was time for him to leave. He sunk into the house's foundation and phased he way out to the street.

A thought occurred to him as he surfaced in the parking garage of Harbor Regional hospital. Why wait to lose his paycheck? He could go right to the source and find out if there was something about Dani's situation he needed to know.

He phased back into the concrete. Instead of heading home, he made a sharp left turn at the Fashion Square mall, bypassed the Arena, and phased a few minutes later into the Blackwoods' sunroom. Through screened walls, the sounds of frogs and other critters echoed from the expansive back yard leading to their private dock on Mystic Bay.

A fuzzy black shadow rubbed against his ankles. "Evening, Eight-ball. Too lazy to hunt tonight?"

He picked up the black cat for a quick cuddle, but Eight-ball purred his demand for scratchies. Nik knew better than to phase with a cat in hand. The one time he'd tried it he'd ended up with a few deep lacerations. Instead, he took the long way around by opening the back door and letting himself into the kitchen.

His mother worked around-the-clock even on her most relaxed days, with Thomas matching her hour for hour, but he expected Garrett, their long-time butler, would be fast asleep.

The faint sound of voices wafted through the kitchen. Nik headed for the entertainment room and found the door ajar. Inside, Hannah Quinn sat on the couch talking to his younger brother, Cory, whose face filled a computer screen. The squeak of the door's hinges caught Hannah's attention. She looked over to see Nik standing there and started to lean forward. Nik opened the door a little farther as he motioned for her to stay put.

"Thomas?" he mouthed silently.

"Office," she whispered back.

Nik nodded and backed out of the room. His heart ached for the two of them. Hannah still sported bandages from the injuries she'd sustained before the quarry raid, but she'd healed Cory before Thunder City brought the hammer down on their relationship. The two of them weren't allowed to have any physical contact at all until they could prove they had control over their Alt powers. Not that the rules stopped Thunder City from buzzing with excitement over their newest Alts, but few truly understood the power either of them wielded. Especially, Hannah. Nik let out a tired sigh. On top of tracking Fagin, he still needed to read the latest reports on the fallout of the raid.

That would have to keep until tomorrow. Or rather, later today, judging by the three a.m. chime of the grandfather clock in the hallway.

Nik gave Eight-ball a last cuddle before releasing the cat outside of Thomas's office. He knocked quietly, but firmly, to make sure Thomas could hear him.

"Come in," his stepfather called.

Surprise set Thomas to blanking his computer screen as Nik walked into the room. Nik didn't blame him. As the oldest son, Nik had survived his parent's divorce when he was five and his mom's marriage to her second husband when he was six. Before Cory was even born, husband number two had been killed. Fortunately, his mother had the good grace not to bring home any other men until she met Thomas. Even then, Thomas pretty much left Nik, Evan, and Alek alone unless there was a situation involving Cory (whom he'd adopted), the house, or T-CASS business.

"It's a bit of a late night for you, Nik. What's wrong?"

Nik took the proffered chair next to Thomas's desk. "I have a question for you. About one of your clients."

Thomas leaned back in his chair, his face already closed before Nik even asked. "I don't talk about my clients, Nik. Any more than you would talk about your own or your father's."

It was a bad start to the conversation. His feelings for Dani were still too new and too strong. Thoughts of Dani in danger overwhelmed his best judgement. He needed to try again.

"You're right. I'm sorry. Let me try again. I met Daniella Rose yesterday. I've known her since we were kids. Mom and Dad know her parents. We grew up together, but I haven't seen her since we graduated from high school. Back then, she was a different person. She didn't have many friends, but I do know she ran into trouble toward end of our senior year.

"I've also been to her home in the Fargrounds. I saw the security system and recognized it as one of your custom jobs.

"All I want to know is: do you feel in your expert opinion that there is an active threat against her? Should I be as worried as I already am?»

One of the qualities Nik had to admire about Thomas was the man's ability to listen to you when you talked. He never interrupted. Even now, he sat there looking at Nik with his arms draped over his stomach, rocking slightly back-and-forth.

"What sort of system do you think you saw?" his voice casual, non-accusatory.

"The grand package: multiple cameras, glass-break, motion sensor, panic button, and I'm assuming twenty-four hour monitoring. Stuff I would expect around here, not in a tiny cape in the Fargrounds."

Thomas didn't respond. Instead he stood up and grabbed a glass from the curio where he kept some fine liquors. He poured himself two fingers of what Nik suspected was brandy — Thomas's preferred drink

— before raising the bottle to Nik, offering him some of the contents.

Nik declined with a raised hand. He'd had enough to drink for one evening.

Thomas reseated himself. "If I'm understanding the situation, your interest in Daniella is personal, not professional."

Nik hesitated, but what was the point? It wasn't like everyone in T-CASS wouldn't be able to figure out he and Serena weren't getting back together, the next time either one of them reported in for a shift.

"You're correct," Nik said. "Serena and I gave it one last shot, but decided it was a waste of our time to keep trying to rekindle something that died a long time ago." Except this time he'd been the one to walk away, but Thomas didn't need to know the details. "I needed to contact Dani on behalf of a client and things proceeded from there. When I saw your system in her home, I became concerned."

"Why don't you just ask her?" Thomas took a sip of his drink before placing his glass on the desk to once more lean back and study Nik.

Yeah, Nik, why don't you just ask her? "It's too soon for that and I don't want her to think I'm investigating her."

"Aren't you?"

Thomas would make one hell of an interrogator. "No, I'm not. I mean, yes, I ran a skiptrace so I could locate her. She wasn't difficult to find, but she'd moved a number of times since I last saw her. That's not the same as what you're implying. I'm not investigating her because I think she's doing anything wrong. I don't want her to think I'm suspicious of her."

"For what it's worth Nik, I don't blame you for

your concern." Thomas took another sip of brandy. "A young woman with a past could be touchy about someone poking their nose into her business. I'll even admit that when the sales department contacted me about some concerns they had about her request for the grand package, as you called it, I made a few inquires myself. I wanted to see if there was anything else I could do to ease her mind concerning whatever was causing her to purchase such an extensive system. I don't need a reputation for making money by scaring young women. But, at the end of the day, Doctor Rose knew what she wanted and could afford it, so we gave it to her. She's not an Alt, and not subject to the agreement Catherine signed with Thunder City, so my inquiry went no further."

"Officially —" Nik prompted, with more hope in his voice than he'd intended. He knew Thomas often played in the gray areas of the law, sometimes on behalf of T-CASS, sometimes for his clients, and other times just to keep himself one step ahead of the competition. Nothing like what he used to do before he married Catherine — or so he had claimed over the years.

"And, unofficially." Thomas sat up, bringing the conversation to a close. "I don't have time to chase after ghosts, pardon my pun. Doctor Rose is as secure as I can make her. If there's a security breach on her property, my employees will know about it and will know how to handle it."

There was nothing else Nik could do. He stood up and reached to shake Thomas's hand. It wasn't right to expect Thomas to cross his own ethical line to soothe Nik's concern. Nik couldn't say he'd have reacted with more grace if the roles had been reversed.

"What do you intend to do?" Thomas followed Nik

to the door. "Will you pursue this or let it drop?"

Nik paused, his hand on the doorknob. He never dealt well with vulnerability, and vulnerability sprouted from a lack of knowledge. Not knowing who was threatening Dani drew him to her even more. He could still taste her wine-flavored kisses on his lips. He wanted to race right back to her house and feel her body pressed against his once more. "I don't know. What would you do in my place?"

"In your place, I would take what I already knew about the young lady, analyze it, give it a good hard think, and see where that leads me." This time Thomas hesitated. "One of the first questions I would ask myself is what sort of security Dani used when she lived in Star Haven? Then I would go talk her. Sooner rather than later."

Nik gave his stepfather a hard stare. Thomas was giving him a clue. One that he intended to follow up on. *Sooner rather than later*, Nik repeated to himself as he gave Thomas a half-wave and phased into the wall. The man was right. Thomas had handed him a key, and Nik intended to use it.

~★~

Dani yawned as she waved good-bye to the security guard at the exit to Generation Med. He gave her a nod. The man might be good-looking, but Dani found him sober and serious and completely uninteresting. There was a time when it wouldn't have mattered to her whether or not a man was interesting, but age and maturity had upgraded her taste. She had a taste for Nik Blackwood, a taste she'd yearned for even as she dated other men while believing Nik would always remain out of reach. He was in her grasp now and she had no intentions of letting him get away.

The open-air Generation Med parking lot didn't offer much in the way of cover. No matter what time of day she arrived, she always managed to find the last open parking spot farthest from the emergency security posts. Given the neighborhood in which Generation Med resided and the loss of sunlight in autumn, Dani made it a point to keep an extra eye out for unaccountable shadows and other creepy things.

Despite the lack of sleep last night, her extra eye still raised the hairs on the back of her neck. She had just passed a pickup truck parked opposite her compact coupe. The judgmental side of her, the side she fought with a passion, made a quick deposit in her brain. Who at Generation Med would own a pickup truck? Most of her colleagues were plugged-in hipsters or millennial geeks, always looking for the newest fashions and coolest gadgets. The truck could belong to one of the guards, but their shifts started before she arrived and their cars would be closer to the building. Same thing with the janitorial service.

Instinct took over. Dani stopped short of her car and pulled out her compact, letting vain and wicked come out to play. Anyone looking at her from a distance would think she was checking her hair and makeup in case she got pulled over by a cute cop on the way home. Always concerned with her outsides instead of her insides, as Grandma Carmelita would gripe. Well, the old bat knew how to push Dani's buttons until the day Dani stopped caring and pushed back. Offended, Grandma Carmelita packed up and left the house that same day. It was the last time she saw her grandmother alive, thank heavens.

Dani spotted menace number one slipping out from under the pickup while menace number two hopped out of the truck bed. Hum, one of the darlings carried a pack under his arm. Really? This was more than a purse snatching.

If she didn't time this right, it wouldn't work. She snapped her compact closed. She had made a deal with one of the security guards to hold her purse in the security suite while she was in the building. It was a routine she stuck to every day, depositing her purse and picking it back up again, ensuring that her purse — and its contents — never passed through the building's security perimeter.

Three...two...one. Just as the twin menaces reached for her, Dani used her small stature to her advantage. She ducked under their arms and plowed her body backwards, taking them by surprise. Before they recovered, she had her Smith & Wesson in her hands and fired it over their heads.

"Freeze, assholes," she said with as much sweetness as lemonade on a hot summer's day.

From behind her, she heard clapping. "Nice trick, little lady. Just not fancy enough."

Dani didn't bother to turn her head. She didn't have to. She knew that beautiful baritone voice better than anyone in Thunder City.

Fagin didn't stay behind her. He moseyed passed her to the two thugs he'd hired. Boys really. Fagin always caught them while they were young, impressionable, and angry. Then, he trained them up and wove them into his network. Just like he had done with Dodger all those years ago.

She could see him now. How could such a beautiful voice belong to such an ugly man? His hair was shorter now, with more salt than pepper. Prison had added an extra left turn to a nose that always had more zags than zigs. The left turn accentuated his long, horse-like face covered by wrinkled skin.

"I can already see, Daniella, that you are going to be a challenge. I suppose asking you to join me before your security friends show up is too much to ask?" Fagin held out a meaty, left hand to her.

"I'm afraid I'll have to decline," she said, her gun steadier than her heart. She could hear sirens in the background. Security had heard her shot.

Fagin shrugged as he turned his back on her and started to walk away. "Let's go, boys. The hunt just became more interesting."

Menace one did as he was told. Menace two stared at her as if he wanted to try and charge her again.

"Please," she said. "I need the practice."

His right foot shuffled a half inch forward. Then the ground exploded next to him, knocking him on his ass, and his pack spilled open to reveal a syringe, cloth, and rope. Ghost in all his costumed glory loomed over the jackass.

"Is there a problem here?" Nik dared the three men to challenge him.

Dani's heart skipped a beat. Oh, how she loved it when her man took charge, looking all sexy in his uniform.

Fagin stopped in place and slumped his shoulders — in exasperation, no doubt — before he turned to face the enemy.

"Nothing happening here, Ghost. Just a little misunderstanding."

"And, just what sort of misunderstanding would cause a woman to pull a gun on you, Fagin?"

"The honest kind." Fagin removed his sunglasses. "The little lady has a flat tire."

Only then did Dani notice that the tire on her coupe was, in fact, flat. Fagin must have sliced the tire, just in case she kicked up a fuss and made it to her car. He always planned ahead like that. Dodger used to help him plan.

"My boys and I wanted to offer her a ride, but she... overreacted."

Sirens still wailed in the background. Dani might have to go to the police station, no matter what, to explain why she had discharged a gun in an open parking lot. She could accuse Fagin of accosting her, but the charge would lead to nothing. It never had... until the last time.

"The gentleman is right, Ghost. It was all just a misunderstanding." She slipped the Smith & Wesson back into her purse just as the police arrived.

Ghost backed away from the menaces until he stood beside her, his eyes not leaving Fagin. "Are you sure, Dani?"

The concern in his voice tempted her to say *no*, she wasn't sure, but saying *no* came with extreme risk. Fagin wasn't stupid. If anyone could figure out that Dani was once Dodger, it would be Fagin. Ghost wanted to nail him almost as bad as she did, but saying *yes* was the safer option.

"I'm sure, Ghost. It's fine. He did nothing wrong. It was all just a misunderstanding."

Dani watched Fagin and his two thugs walk off the lot, her luck following them. She stepped closer to Nik as her heart slowed, her hand finding its way to his lower back for a supportive rub. He didn't look at her, his eyes fixed on his retreating targets.

T-CASS always worked in groups of at least two or more, but tonight Nik was alone. Fagin was sure to read something into that. If Fagin hadn't known Nik was following him, he did now. By walking into Fagin's crosshairs on his own, Nik had given Fagin the leverage he needed to use Dani against Nik, and vice versa. A hundred different horrible scenarios, most of Dodger's own design, flashed through her mind. She had to stop Fagin and she had to do it soon.

Dani's free hand stroked her purse, bulging with her gun inside. Vain and wicked would have its day.

CHAPTER FIVE

"Nik.»

No response. Oh, dear. Nik sat half turned on his side of the booth, stirring his steaming bowl of soup. The steam swirled around his still gloved fingers. His eyes were unfocused, and he was deep in thoughts Dani suspected were not about her. Or rather, he thought about her and why a guy like Fagin would want to kidnap her. Which was not how she wanted Nik thinking about her.

"Ni-ik," she said a little louder, a little sweeter, with an extra syllable to get her point across.

Sky blue eyes looked up as if he had heard her just fine the first time, but hadn't wanted his train of thought interrupted.

"Something on your mind? Or, do you just like ignoring me in favor of a boring bowl of chicken noodle?" She kept her lilt light as a breeze off the harbor on a sunny day. She could lose him right now if he thought for one moment she had a connection with Fagin. Which she didn't. Dani didn't. Dodger was another story altogether.

"We need to discuss why Fagin tried to kidnap you this afternoon," he said.

She sighed, but favored him with a small smile full of

promise and her favorite rose-colored lipstick. "Honey, I already know why Fagin wanted to kidnap me. The only thing we need to discuss is how to tell Robby that he'll have to leave town for a while if he wants my kidney."

Nik jerked upright, as if he'd forgotten about the reason he'd contacted her in the first place. Of course she'd have to leave the city for the transplant.

"You know why he wanted to kidnap you?" He banged his spoon down on the table, the full force of his aggression on her as he leaned over the table to grab her hand. "Why? What's going on that I don't know about?"

"Gently, Nik. This is one of my two favorite hands." She plucked at his fingers to loosen his grip.

"I'm sorry." He let go, with a proper apologetic look. "You scared me this afternoon. I stop by Generation Med to ask you to dinner, only to find you standing there in the parking lot fending off three men twice your size, and with a gun in your hand."

"Which I handled quite well, all things considered." She picked up her fork to spear a floret of broccoli sitting next to her Reuben. She could at least try to eat something healthy while calming down Nik. "There was no reason to be scared."

"No reason to be scared," Nik repeated. "Fagin, Thunder City's nightmare, targets you for a kidnapping and you say there's no reason to be scared."

She let the sarcasm roll past her. It was best to let the man get it out of his system before she talked reason with him. Besides, the broccoli was cooked to perfection. No reason to let it go to waste. Not with the Reuben going to her waist in a few minutes.

Nik slammed himself back into the booth hard

enough to catch the attention of the other diners around them. A strapping man in a skintight T-CASS uniform would catch anyone's attention on a good day, but in Thunder City most folks had the good grace not to interfere with an Alt if he looked like he was on duty. Tonight, Nik looked like thunder, which only made him sexier and more attention-grabbing.

Dani ate in silence for a few minutes while Nik watched her.

"So, tell me why you think Fagin wanted to kidnap you."

"He wants to stop my research." It had taken a while to calm herself down and think through Fagin's motivations from his point of view. He didn't know about her Alt ability. He didn't know she had once been his Artful Dodger, his right hand man and lover. Dani had always expected that he would figure it out some day. Someone would put two and two together and Fagin would come after Dodger for setting him up and stealing his money. Dani never figured Fagin would care about Dani, so her research was the only other explanation. "I found a cure for blitz addiction. That's why I joined Generation Med. Well, one of the reasons. They want to support my research and start clinical trials. Fagin wants to stop the research because I could put a huge dent in his operation."

"Makes sense," Nik said. She could see him processing the implications of her research, the cute way his eyes shifted back and forth, as if he were reading his own thoughts. Adorable. "How does it work? Your cure?"

She shrugged. "I wrote about it in a paper I published last year. It involves increasing the number of antibodies used to attack blitz before it enters the brain. Antibodies are not infinite. The goal of my research is to prevent the addict from continuing to increase the amount of blitz he ingests to get high. The idea is to create an implant that will release as many antibodies as needed to attack the blitz before it enters the brain."

Nik had that deep in thought look again. "So if it works, blitz addiction will be neutralized forever because the implant will keep releasing antibodies every time the addict ingests more blitz."

Dani shrugged. "If people want a cure, it'll be available to them. You can't force people to give up their addiction if they don't want to."

"If it's the difference between a cure and jail — "

"There will always be new addicts, Nik. My cure is specific to blitz. Don't think a guy like Fagin is going to disappear just because I poisoned his well. He'll change his colors, switch his operation and sell something else."

"Televisions would be nice," Nik muttered.

Dani laughed, licking a drop of Thousand Island off her fingertip. Still no reaction from Nik. Damn, he was a tough nut to crack when he was on a case.

"Now that we know why Fagin wants you, it'll be just a matter of time before he slips up. We'll arrest him and put him away for good. You won't have to leave."

Even to her ears, Nik's words sounded hollow. Perhaps even desperate. Oh, this sweet man with the tender heart didn't want her to leave. Her own heart went all pitter patter at the sentiment.

Laughter from the booth behind her distracted Dani from her thoughts. She raised her voice to make sure her man could hear her. "Let's not kid ourselves, Nik. Fagin's network and power in Thunder City may have diminished since his conviction, but if you think he hasn't continued to operate from behind bars, then you're a fool."

"I'm not a fool." Nik ripped open a small package of saltines to add to his soup. Dani could almost pity Fagin if Nik ever got his hands on the drug dealer. "I know what he's been up to, but no one's been able to prove it."

Dani wiped the edge of her mouth with her napkin. "And, that's the problem. You can't play by the rules with Fagin and expect to win."

"We won last time. We put him in prison.»

"For less than a decade," Dani said. "Convicted of possession of a quarter pound of unprocessed blitz, not because of the warehouse full of the stuff you uncovered. Not for any of the people he murdered. If you had a solid case against him for any of that, he'd still be in the city prison."

If he'd been an Alt it would have been different. Rocklin Prison, which held the worst Chaos Alts, would have prevented Fagin from continuing his operation, but without a proven Alt ability, Fagin had remained in the regular city prison with the other Norms. Security was tight, but Fagin would always find ways around it.

"C'mon, honey." This time Dani reached out to rub the back of Nik's hand. "Let's finish dinner and head back to your place. We'll have some more of that lovely wine and forget our troubles. Tomorrow morning, I'll explain the situation to the Generation Med board. They're going to have fits about security, but that's not my department and not my problem. By tomorrow afternoon, I'll be safe and secure in a hospital outside of Thunder City. Robby will get his kidney and you'll get to feed me cherry-flavored gelatin while I recover."

She hated the defeated look on Nik's face. The look

that said Nik would wrack his brains to try and find
another way to keep her safe here in Thunder City.
Unlike Dani, Nik wouldn't leave the city of his birth.
After the transplant, she'd have to make a decision
whether or not to risk her heart for a city that never
promised her anything and delivered nothing but pain.

~★~

Not even several hours of heart-pumping sex could
distract Nik from the need to keep Dani safe. No matter
how many kisses he used to try and convince her to
stay with him, she refused to move into his penthouse.

"I have security, Nik," Dani had said. "Security I paid
for. It'll keep Fagin at bay."

He gave in only so she wouldn't fight him when
he insisted on escorting her home again. This time he
didn't bother with the front door. He phased her into
the middle of her living room. No need to turn off
Thomas's security net. Nik knew his way around the
system so he wouldn't trip any wires, and Thomas's
programs auto-loaded Nik's profile into every system
in the city. Nik could get in and out of buildings no
matter what security Thomas provided.

It was the unwritten law of the Blackwoods: Keep
Thunder City safe and Thunder City will keep you safe.
They all had to believe that or every bit of Catherine's
work over the years, all of the sacrifices the T-CASS
members made, would be for naught.

That, and Thomas liked to play in the gray areas of
the law. For once, Nik was grateful for his stepfather's
consideration. Otherwise, he'd be fending off whatever
countermeasures Thomas had built into this particular
system. Nik hoped those measures would be enough
for tonight because he'd be back here first thing in the
morning to take Dani to work.

"Nightcap?" Dani waved her hand toward the small wine refrigerator tucked into the corner.

Nik grabbed her hand and pulled her into his arms again. She was like a drug he couldn't get enough of. Her head didn't even reach his chest, and yet the curve of her body against his electrified him, at the same time as it gave his mind a sense of peace. He lowered his chin to kiss the mop of curls piled on top her head. "No. Not tonight. I still have work to do."

He felt her hand slip around his waist to cup his backside. "Well, then, I suggest to you get going, because I have to get my beauty sleep."

His heart raced even faster as she slipped him a saucy wink over her shoulder as she turned to walk toward the stairs. He counted to ten, listening to her footsteps leading up to where he presumed her bedroom was. A powerful need to follow her, to make sure there were no monsters hidden under her bed, almost forced him up the stairs, but he'd seen Dani handle a gun today. She didn't need his protection, any more than she needed him in her bed after they'd spent most of the late afternoon in his.

He waited until he heard water from the shower pour through the pipes before he sunk into the house's foundation and raced away before his heart and his lust could change his mind. It wouldn't have taken much encouragement for him to join her in the shower, but he really did have to earn his keep, so he aimed for the Arena instead.

The overnight shift had already settled into their routine by the time he logged into the system. Thomas's set of worker bees, so-called because of the bright yellow polo shirts they wore along with their black pants, sat at their work stations around the perimeter of the darkened oval-shaped main hall. Above his head, huge television screens streamed the local news broadcasts from Thunder City and Star Haven. In the center of the hall, two sets of T-CASS teams in colorful uniforms sat around a levitating table waiting for an alert that would send them into action.

Nik knew there were other work stations in the back conference rooms, so he headed in that direction. If he was lucky, Thomas's advanced team would have left for the day and he would use one of their stations.

"Nik, can I talk to you for a moment, please?"

Nik stopped, but hesitated to turn around as the worry for Dani's safety dribbled out of his heart and left only dread behind. He should have known Serena would stay past her shift. She always stayed past her shift.

He couldn't ignore her though, couldn't pretend he hadn't heard her. So, he turned to face his ex-fiancée, ex-girlfriend, ex-lover. She had been all that and more, on and off, since high school. He couldn't ignore her any more than he could ignore their shared past.

Serena stood in a neutral stance, hands at her sides. Instead of her bright yellow on-duty uniform with matching barrette in her jet black hair, she wore a simple pair of dark yoga pants and a green Thunder City Tornadoes T-shirt.

"Sure." He motioned her ahead of him, since he didn't know if she was going to take this into her own office or somewhere more private. Serena had taken over from Gavin Harris, Blockhead, as the head of training. It was a huge responsibility, ranging from teaching control to the new Alts in the elementary and middle school systems as their powers manifested, to recruiting alternative humans in high schools to work for T-CASS after they graduated. Her job responsibilities hadn't caused their break-up the second time, but they hadn't helped either.

She led him to her office and closed the door. Like Serena herself, the office appeared as neat and tidy as an unused kitchen. No paper dared litter her desk. Every file folder had its place, every pen was stashed away. He noticed the picture of the two of them at the senior prom no longer sat next to the picture of her parents and siblings. He couldn't blame her for removing it. It didn't take a genius to know how much of her pride he'd damaged in breaking off their third attempt to make their relationship work so soon after the raid. Had it been less than a week since he'd walked away?

"What's this all about?" He sat in the hot seat, the chair next to her desk. Many a young trainee had sat there to get a harsh review of their performance. Serena held a standard higher than T-CASS required for all of her trainees.

"What do you think you're doing, Nik?"

"About what?"

Serena twisted her computer screen around. Nik could tell from a glance it was the *Thunder City Tattler's* web site. It only took a glance to recognize the front page photo of him and Dani dancing at the club. *Ghost dumps Highlight for Mysterious New Woman?* He didn't need to read the rest.

"It looks like I had a fun date. Hardly a reason to call me into your office." He stood to leave. The last person he was going to discuss Dani with was Serena.

"Sit down, Nik. I'm not finished with you yet."

Nik stopped short. For all of their fights and arguments, she'd never talked him like that. He'd also never pulled rank on her before, never let his family ties to the founders of T-CASS color their relationship. He must have done more damage than he thought to put her so far off her game.

Nik fought to keep his voice down as he turned back around to lean over the desk. "I'm *not* one of your trainees, Serena. Don't you dare speak to me like that again."

Her Adam's apple bobbed up and down as she swallowed her own outrage. "I'm sorry, Nik, but this is serious business."

She broke eye contact to click a key on her keyboard. The *Thunder City News-Journal* appeared on the screen. This one showed a screen capture from a security camera: Dani fending off Fagin and his men in the parking lot. Nik's pride in Dani rose up to snuff out his anger. His fear for her safety remained, but it wasn't the near paralyzing fear he felt earlier.

He sighed. "What are you doing, Serena?"

"I'm asking you the same question, Nik. T-CASS has enough problems with the quarry raid investigation. We don't need a security breach."

"What security breach?" he asked. "What are you talking about?"

"I'm talking about you...dating a woman with an arrest record. We can't afford to have you give Star Haven an inroad into T-CASS operations. If they think you're passing information along to a woman with her background. . . ."

"That woman has a name," he snapped.

"I know her name," Serena crossed her arms and looked him directly in the eye. "You couldn't walk through the hallways of Kensington without hearing her name."

Nik stepped back. He needed space to think, room

to get his thoughts in order. He had to separate Nik, a man in love, from Ghost, a man with a responsibility to T-CASS. "I know I hurt you, Serena. Hooking up with you before the raid...it was a mistake. I led you to believe we could make it work. It won't. I'm sorry. Attacking Daniella Rose based on nothing more than high school hijinks is beneath you and it's not going to help T-CASS."

Serena stepped around the desk, violating his personal space. "You think this is about our relationship? Nik, that's hardly the problem. The problem is her record."

"She doesn't have a record. The judge dismissed her case." Serena should have known that. She would have known that if she'd truly investigated Daniella, like Nik had before he'd contacted her.

"It doesn't matter." Serena returned to her seat behind the desk. "Daniella's arrest still made the papers. Her past will reflect on your present, Nik. If you keep seeing her, her past will reflect on T-CASS. If you have any hopes of taking control of this organization, you can't get involved with people like her."

This was the crux of their problem. Serena lived and breathed for T-CASS and couldn't understand why Nik didn't join her. His refusal to commit every waking moment to his work for T-CASS annoyed her. The first time they'd broken off their relationship, he had thought she'd hung her star on marrying into the Blackwood family so she could shine next him. But in reality, Serena had deserved every bit of praise she'd gotten for her dedication to T-CASS. She modeled herself after Captain Spectacular, his mother, and never understood how Nik could split his loyalty between his long-divorced parents.

"Mom never promised to let me take over T-CASS

when she retires." He'd said it before, but he could see Serena gearing up for another argument.

"Stop being so naïve. The expectation is Catherine will hand you the reins sometime in the next five years."

Where the hell had she gotten that information? "I can't control other people's expectations."

"And, we're getting off track." Serena stopped, closed her eyes and took a deep breath. "Daniella Rose is bad news, Nik. She always was."

"So, nothing she's done in the past ten years counts for anything? Not her education? Not her unblemished employment record?"

"People don't change that much. Look at her." Serena clicked the screen again to increase the size of the image. "That's Fredek Varga — Fagin — but I don't need to tell you that."

"He's targeted her because of her research at Generation Med. I'm handling her security."

"Which T-CASS has not authorized you to do, by the way," Serena said.

Damn, she was on a roll today. This was why it had never worked between them. Serena never backed down. She would fight long after she'd won or lost an argument. Their last and final argument as a couple had been just like this. Nik had realized that he was following in the footsteps of his parents. The endless string of arguments over everything. As a child, he would phase into the walls and listen. Then, he'd wander the grounds of the estate, depressed and unable to understand why he couldn't get his parents to stop shouting. By the time his father moved out of their house, Nik had come to believe that the arguments were a normal part of any family. It took time, and many friendships outside of the family, to learn the right way to argue with someone you loved. Some folks never learned that lesson.

"Regardless," Serena continued. "This is proof she hasn't changed as much as you seem to think she has. Why would Fagin, a known blitz distributor, care about one time blitz addict if they had no ties."

Nik lost his patience. "One: she was never an addict. She got caught at a frat party where blitz was present. The judge laughed the prosecutor out of the courtroom when she tried to prosecute Dani's case. Two: Her research is provocative. If she can stop blitz addiction cold — that's a damn good reason for someone like Fagin to target her."

He could see he'd caught Serena off guard.

"I didn't know about her research."

Nik hoped Serena's change of tone meant she would leave the argument alone. "She only published one paper, right before she left Star Haven. If you were really interested in learning about what Daniella has been up to, you would have read it."

"Which raises more questions. Why did she leave so suddenly? She could have gotten an assistant professorship. She could have gotten tenure. Why head back to Thunder City for the private sector? Why now?"

He should have known Serena wouldn't back down, but instead change tactics. It didn't matter. He was done. "You'll have to ask her, Serena. I'm not going to."

"Don't force me to start a formal investigation, Nik."

"Then don't." Nik only had enough emotional energy to shrug at Serena's threat. "You have nothing to investigate. T-CASS won't allow you to investigate my personal life based on your jealousy. The whole purpose of T-CASS is to allow alternative humans our right to live, work, and form personal relationships just like normal humans."

"All of our personal relationships are being scrutinized, Nik. Hannah Quinn's insistence on maintaining a relationship with Scott Grey..."

"Cory. His name is Cory Blackwood." He put strong emphasis on Blackwood.

"Whatever he's calling himself this week." She waved her hand as if she were dismissing a fly and not Nik's brother. "Their relationship cannot continue without oversight, yet she's threatening to walk away from us... from Thunder City, from T-CASS, if she's not allowed to continue to see him. It's causing havoc in the Alt community. She's creating dissent between T-CASS and the Neuts. Neutrals have always challenged the security protocols we put in place to keep untrained Alts from causing harm to themselves and to others. You dating Daniella is only going to create more scrutiny. People will start questioning our integrity."

"Norms, you mean. You're worried Daniella will create a scandal that will lend support to the Neuts who want to tear down the safety protocols and tear down T-CASS along with them. That will give the Norms more power every time an Alt causes an accident with their powers."

"Yes."

Nik counted to ten in hopes of finding a polite way to counter Serena's argument. He couldn't. "You're a fool, Serena. If a Norm like Daniella and an Alt like me can't fall in love without creating havoc for T-CASS, then maybe T-CASS should be torn down."

Serena choked on his words, her brown eyes widening at the horror of what he had said. "You don't mean that."

Nik turned and walked away.

CHAPTER SIX

Dani set the alarm on her house before she stepped outside. As sophisticated as the system was, it didn't take the place of personal caution. She gave her front yard and the yards of her neighbors a careful visual and auditory scan with the small jack that had come with her security system. Her heightened awareness made every sound, every shadow a potential threat, but she had to be sure. Even in the black of night, Carraro's system would tell her if something was amiss.

Something was definitely out of place. Underneath the green SUV next door someone watched her. Good. She slipped the device and her phone into her pocket and jogged down her driveway. At the end, she turned left, trying not to trip over the hem of the oversized track suit she wore. In her pocket, the device vibrated once. She was being followed, but she didn't hit the alarm just yet.

While she had showered, she'd also listened for telltale signs of Nik leaving, but she hadn't heard anything. He must have phased through the house to get outside. Did he sneak upstairs to get a peek of her in the shower before he left? Probably not. Straight-laced Nik Blackwood would never do anything so crass. He didn't have to because he'd already seen her naked. Why, just this afternoon he'd chased her naked through his penthouse and into his bed before bringing her home. What a merry time that had been, but thinking about it distracted her from keeping her pursuer close, but not too close.

Dani hadn't expected Fagin would come after her. Dodger, yes. The damage Dodger had inflicted on Fagin's operation, after the judge released her, had sent Fagin to jail and disrupted if not destroyed his network. She had assumed Fagin's need for vengeance would override everything else, but she'd been wrong. His need to reestablish his network took priority over vengeance. At least until he could find Dodger.

In Star Haven, hiding Dodger had served to keep Dani safe in a community that hated Alts. Her first year in Star Haven had woken her up to how much Thunder City Alts owed Catherine Blackwood and her fight to create a safe city for Alts to live in, a city where Alts didn't have to hide their abilities or wear masks to use them.

It also hadn't taken long for her to realize that by never shifting, never allowing the male side of herself out to play, she had created an emotional black hole. For all of her feminine traits, a part of Daniella enjoyed being a male. All of the traits other people remarked on about Daniella — her confidence, her passion, her driven attitude — all remained unremarked on by others when they met her as a male.

That was why she created Daniel. Daniel was her compromise. Whereas Dodger reached six foot seven and possessed the muscles of a professional bodybuilder, Daniel was about six foot two with big enough muscles to win a fist fight if he had to — not that Daniel ever started them. Daniel looked like your sexy next door neighbor who would be happy to take your dog out for a walk. Dodger would scare the dog.

Now she had to try and get Fagin to chase Dodger and not Daniella. If she could keep Fagin on the chase for Dodger, a man who had no real identity, maybe he would leave Daniella alone. At least until she could get past her kidney donation to Robby.

Cat and mouse never had it so tough. Time to make a left turn.

Behind her, she could hear the light *flop-flop* of sneakers following her. Her S&W rested in a shoulder holster and flopped against her chest since she had to keep the strap loose.

One more mile to go. The Fargrounds had its share of police patrols this late at night, but if anyone wondered why a single, tiny woman was out jogging this late, they didn't stop to ask.

Up ahead, the Mystic Bay Health Recovery Center loomed. Unlike the rest of the Fargrounds, the building had sufficient lighting and security despite its bland, brick exterior. Dani needed the light, but she didn't need the attention.

She picked up speed just long enough to lose her tail at the next right turn down the alley between the building and the gas station next door. It took her a full twenty seconds for her to change enough to make her follower see what she wanted him to see. She couldn't wait to complete the change to Dodger and still time this operation to her advantage, so she shifted to Daniel instead.

Now that her track suit fit properly, she sauntered out to the corner of the building and leaned back, chin up and balls out. The tail ran right past Daniel. He stopped short at the corner of the gas station, his stance confused as he craned his neck around.

"Looking for someone?" Daniel asked, hoping his voice didn't squeak as his vocal cords continued to shift.

"Yeah." The tail approached Daniel without hesitation. "A girl. She just jogged past here."

Daniel flexed his muscles, a gesture of indifference as well strength. While he stretched, he stepped off the curb. The street lights now made his face visible as well as his height.

Daniel could now see the tail's face. He was one of the boys who had tried to kidnap Daniella from Gen Med's parking lot.

"Saw her. She headed north." Daniel jerked his chin that general direction.

The tail squinted at Daniel, taking in the long brown hair, pulled back into a man bun, his firm jaw, his better than average size. There were only two reasons why a man like Daniel would be standing outside a drug treatment clinic so late at night: either the clinic had hired him to supplement their security, or he was a dealer looking for stragglers he could hook before they made it inside the clinic's walls. Those in the midst of treatment made the best customers if a dealer could play on their insecurities.

"Thanks, man." The kid didn't back away. "Do I know you?"

"You're one of Fagin's boys?" Daniel made it clear it wasn't really a question.

"I ain't no boy."

Typical youth – all bluster, no brains. "My apologies. Tell Fagin, Dodger sends his love."

Daniel almost laughed as the tail's eyes went wide with recognition. Either Dodger's reputation remained intact after all of these years, or Fagin was talking about him to his new crew. Daniel doubted Fagin had anything pleasant to say about his former lover.

The tail backed away toward the corner, then turned and ran in the direction Daniel had sent him. Daniel waited until the tail crossed the street and disappeared around the next building. By morning, Fagin would know Dodger was still in town.

At best, he would forget about Daniella and start chasing Dodger. More than likely, Daniel had managed to split Fagin's attention. The more Daniel/Daniella could split Fagin's attention, the more mistakes Fagin would make. Mistakes Daniella could take advantage of before Fagin caught her.

And then what? The only way to end this is to kill him.

Daniel shifted back to Daniella before she reached her front yard. If she killed Fagin, the problem would go away, never to return, but it could create an even bigger problem. Nik would have to know the truth about her past. She would have to tell him about her ability to shift. He would have to report what he knew about her to T-CASS. T-CASS would demand that she register with Thunder City. T-CASS would also demand she prove her ability to control her shift.

She had gone to school with at least half the members of the current T-CASS roster. They would remember the rumors, some true, but most not. She had no interest in working with those people. She had no interest in T-CASS beyond Nik. Upstairs, she stripped off the oversized sweat shirt and pants and collapsed into bed.

Dani wished Nik occupied her bed so she could curl up next to his warm body and feel safe in his arms. Given the opportunity, she would have stayed curled up next to him in his bed until morning. Nik's bed was much bigger and far more luxurious than her own and would have made for an easy rest before she headed to work. Unfortunately, sleeping — really sleeping — in a bed with a man wasn't as easy for her as it was for others. The last time she'd loved a man enough to spend the night, she'd shifted in her sleep. Even though she'd warned her fiancé at the time that it might happen, he still freaked and broke off their engagement.

Just as well. Her ex would never have agreed to leave Star Haven because of the Alt ban. He loved her, but not enough to disrupt his life for her. Four pints of ice cream and a three day movie marathon in her apartment had dulled the pain of rejection, if not cured it. Maybe after Generation Med released her blitz addiction cure on the world, she could work on a vaccine for heartache.

If Nik loves you, you won't need it.

Oh, what a lovely thought. If Nik loved her, she wouldn't need a lot of things, but first she'd have to tell him about Daniel and Dodger. Having to explain to the man she loved about her shift was hard enough. Having to explain to the man she loved that the man he had hunted all through high school, the man whom he had held responsible for releasing blitz into the Thunder City school system, who had destroyed lives, and started a murderous drug war, was actually the women he was bedding — that took moxy even she didn't have right now.

No one would believe, much less understand, the depth of her regret about her actions back then. Dodger was born out her own desperate need to be loved. Fagin found Dodger attractive, and Dodger never told Fagin about Daniella. The fact that Fagin never asked Dodger for his real name should have been Daniella's first clue to Fagin's indifference. Instead, the newly dubbed "Dodger" fell for Fagin's charm. The drug lord took the brazen young man under his wing, nurtured him in a way her parents should have, but didn't. He guided Dodger, in his own twisted way. He gave Dodger confidence. He gave Dodger an outlet for Daniella's rage. Through Fagin's unbridled violence, the vain and wicked girl could always win the day.

Fagin turned Dodger into the best dealer in Thunder City, then abandoned him at the time Dodger needed him the most. Daniella had used her rapid shift during the frat party raid to prevent the cops from connecting Dodger to Fagin. Better to have them think the spoiled debutante was slumming with the frat boys, rather than trying to become just like them — doing normal stuff young men do in college. She never forgot those long days she spent in jail waiting for someone to bail her out. She ended up having to call her parents because Fagin had already replaced Dodger. Dodger, it seemed, had grown too old to hold Fagin's interest.

Thunder City would never forgive her for what she had done. Nik...she could only hope that Nik would forgive her when she told him the truth, and she *would tell him*.

Dani flopped over and clutched her pillow closer, holding tight onto her wish.

I wish I may, I wish I might, have this wish I wish tonight.

She promised to tell Nik soon, if only he would love her back as much as she loved him. She continued to sing to herself as she fell into a deep sleep.

~★~

Nik did Detective Trell the courtesy of knocking on his car window before he phased into the passenger seat. He'd learned the hard way not to surprise an armed cop back when he was still a Goob in training. The first ever Goob in training, in fact. Only luck had saved Nik from Officer Trell's bullet, but the police car window had needed to be replaced. The two had worked together often since then.

"I figured you'd phase your way here at some point," Trell said, not even turning his eyes away from the building he surveilled. The years had thinned the man's slicked back brown hair, but he still looked like he could handle whatever threat the Fargrounds tossed at him.

"Isn't staking out a building overnight beneath your pay grade?" Nik snarked back. He'd already had an early morning start getting Dani to work. She'd insisted on driving and drove just like she danced — with wild abandon. Nik tried relax now that she was safe inside the walls of Generation Med. The early morning sun attempted to brighten the downtrodden tenement, but it did nothing to ease Nik's fear for Dani.

"Not staking anything out," Trell said. "I'm waiting for Claire to pack up the last of her art supplies. T-CASS found her a nicer place uptown. Now that she's on the payroll, she can afford better than this. I'm giving her a ride."

Claire the clairvoyant, as she was informally known. She wouldn't get a moniker until the public bestowed one on her. T-CASS was carefully handling how they rolled out their newest member to the public. Between Hannah, Cory, and Claire, the abilities harnessed by T-CASS made the organization more powerful than ever before. Claire was still in training, however, and Hannah... Nik bit back Serena's criticisms. If Hannah continued to play a high-stakes game of chicken with

T-CASS it wouldn't end well for any of them. After Nik dealt with Fagin, he'd sit down and have a serious off-the-record conversation with both Hannah and Cory. Separately, if necessary.

"I'm glad you're keeping an eye on Claire," Nik said.

Trell nodded. "Because of our history together, she's more comfortable working with the police department than with T-CASS, but the more exposure she has to other Alts, the better off she'll be. But, you're not here to talk about Claire, are you?"

Nik leaned back, letting the rising sun warm his face. "No. I'm here to ask if you've had any hits on Fagin's whereabouts."

"So far, nothing." Trell sipped his coffee. "I pulled a list of the places he used for his operation prior to his arrest, but he appears to be avoiding his past haunts. He's gathering the usual around him. A whole new crew. His old guard is either still in prison or dead. Except for the incident with Daniella Rose, we have nothing. Any chance you can talk her into filing a report?"

"Nope," Nik said. "Not for lack of trying."

Trell laughed. "I'll bet you did."

Crap. Trell, and probably the entire police force, had seen the *Tattler* and *News-Journal* reports.

"If what you told me is true," Nik swallowed back his annoyance over the gossip, "and Fagin wants to shut down Doctor Rose's research before he sets up his new network, then we're going to be in for a long wait. Rose hired Carraro's security company. She's locked in tight — at least when she's at home."

"I don't know about that." Trell rolled down his window and waved. The front door to the building had opened and a blond woman walked toward the car with a canvas, stretched and primed for painting, under one arm and a small tote bag in the other. "Fagin has cash. Dodger may have stolen all of Fagin's money, but crews don't work on credit. Maybe Dodger missed something. Fagin's getting support from somewhere or someone."

Yes, but from whom? Nik didn't answer Trell out loud. Instead he phased out of the car and reappeared right next to Claire. "Let me take that for you."

Though they hadn't formally met, Claire must have recognized Nik even though he wasn't in uniform. She relinquished the tote to Nik as Trell walked over to take the canvas.

"I popped the trunk. You can put everything back there," Trell said.

Follow the money. Nik helped Claire secure her belongings. He refused Trell's offer to talk more while he drove Claire to her new apartment and waved good-bye to the two of them. The less Claire knew at this point, the better. Until she'd worked a few T-CASS assignments, Nik didn't want her anywhere near the Fagin case. Which, according to Serena, wasn't even a case at this point. Fagin had paid his dues, served his time, and was a free man.

Nik phased into the tenement, shifted direction, and headed downtown. By all rights, he should head back to the Arena to continue his probe into Fagin's finances, but he didn't relish the thought of running into Serena again. Instead, he headed to his office at his father's detective agency. Right now, the agency didn't have authorization to work on Fagin's case either, but Nik would rather use the agency's resources than return home. Home would only remind him of the way Dani had led him on a very merry — and very naked —

chase last night, around the whole penthouse suite.

Where did such a tiny woman get that kind of energy? She'd scampered over his furniture like an excited kitten escaping with her favorite toy. He captured her only because he phased under the sofa and popped up behind her through the wall. She accused him of cheating.

"You can't blame me for cheating," he'd replied, bending down so his arms could circle her waist, his fingers sliding down to warm and secret places. "Not when you're the prize."

She'd sighed as her head fell back against his shoulder, her curls tickling his ears. He'd pulled her even closer, but it wasn't enough. He wanted her closer, he needed to feel her around him, so he'd tossed her over his shoulder and hauled her off to bed.

Nik sped faster toward his destination. He didn't bother entering through the lobby, or the elevator, or even the front doors to the office suite his father leased. Instead, he popped up in the middle of his office so no one could see him. He needed to get last night's activities off his mind before he embarrassed himself.

Numbers could kill desire faster than a cold shower, so Nik booted up his computer. Who would want to fund Fagin's new network? An hour later he still hadn't advanced beyond a long list of *when hell froze over.* Fagin hadn't remained at the top of the blitz distribution chain for as long as he had by making friends. Nik's own list of enemies fell into the "deceased" or "incarcerated" categories. Of those in the incarcerated category only three might have the brains and the backbone to still have access to their own hidden funds, but how could he prove it? And, why would they have a vested interest in helping Fagin? How could he figure out which one, if any, would do it? How could he uncover any ties, if they existed, without tipping off either Fagin or his funder?

He looked at the string of pictures of his family sitting on the edge of his desk. The nearest one was from his Little League days, with his mother and father after the divorce. A second one was from his high school graduation party with Evan and Alek lifting Nik into the air with their abilities. The third had been taken at his college graduation, with everyone from both sides of the family, including his stepmother and Thomas.

Thomas. Nick sighed and lay his head back on the backrest of his executive chair. Thomas would have no difficulty uncovering any connection between the convicts and Fagin. Would he, though? Thomas played the gray hat hacker when it suited his purpose, whether it benefitted the Blackwoods, T-CASS, or himself. Asking Thomas to play beyond the legal limit required a certain finesse Nik didn't think he had. Still, if it meant putting Fagin away for good and keeping him away from Dani, it was worth asking, wasn't it?

He thought of Dani, so wild and loving, his heart beat off rhythm just thinking of her. She'd been arrested once. What would she think of Nik asking Thomas to break the law on her behalf? He would have to tell her eventually, even if Thomas found nothing. If Thomas even agreed to Nik's request, which he might not.

Nik looked at the family photographs again. He'd never put a picture of Serena next to the pictures of his family. His fingers flexed. He didn't have a picture of Dani yet. He would, though. He'd find a way to get one of them together. He could imagine both of them crammed into a photo booth at the farmer's market, making silly faces while the machine snapped pictures.

Dani would do it too, the sillier the face the better.

He looked at the Little League picture again. His mom had nudged him once or twice about having kids. Like a good son, he'd mentioned it to Serena during one of their better days. Serena had shaken her head. Maybe she saw the look of disappointment on his face, because she quickly amended her statement to not until she was more established in her career. They never talked about kids afterwards.

The sound of a door closing punctuated his thoughts. Voices drifted through the heavy door to his office, followed by the faint sound of a ringing phone. The work day had started. Nik pulled his thoughts back to the problem at hand. If he was going to protect Dani from Fagin, he needed to find the source of Fagin's funding. The strength of T-CASS sprang from their training, their ability to work together.

He would ask Thomas for his help. If Thomas refused, Nik would find another way. He had to. He wanted Dani's picture on his desk.

CHAPTER SEVEN

Dani smiled as she closed the door to the HR department behind her. Generation Med forgave her lateness this morning so she could change her flat tire, but they wouldn't budge on its policy about keeping guns in the building. In all honesty, she couldn't blame them for sticking to the letter of the law. They had, however, promised to set aside a parking space closer to the building just for her. Security would also arrange for an escort to and from the car every day.

A good night's sleep assuaged her worries about telling Nik about her past. He would either forgive her or he wouldn't. If he didn't...there was always ice cream and a movie marathon to ease her broken heart. If Nik didn't love her, she would keep searching for someone who did.

Her phone buzzed from her pocket. She checked the screen, not surprised to see a text message from Nik. Sweet boy was checking to make sure Generation Med was taking good care of her. She texted him back, and invited him to perform a strip search to make sure she hadn't acquired any scratches or bruises during her meeting with HR. His next message suggested a deeper examination. If she kept this up, she'd dash right back out to her car and make a beeline for the detective agency downtown.

She sent him several happy emojis instead before she stepped onto the elevator. Down in her lab, she side-stepped several hunky men moving furniture and equipment around. Lots to admire, but none could beat Nik in the hunky and handsome department. In another lifetime, she would have admired them from afar, but she had work to finish if she wanted the weekend free to entice his-hunkiness back into bed. Maybe the two of them would stay there all weekend. His penthouse sure beat her little cape, but practicality meant she'd have to go home at some point to make up for her lack of maid service.

Her parents had maids and chauffeurs and the like, but Dani had learned how to do her own laundry the second she moved across the Bay.

Her computer burped up a rude message after *she typed in her password:* The user name or password is incorrect. She tried to log on again. Same message. She had never mistyped a password more than once in her life. She requested a new password and tried again. Same message. She grabbed her phone and dialed IT.

"How can we help?" a voice garbled by what sounded like the ocean in the background answered. Generation Med couldn't afford its own IT department yet, so they contracted out to a third party. Who knew where on the planet she was actually calling?

"This is Doctor Daniella Rose at Generation Med. I appear to be locked out of the Generation Med system. I tried to reset my password and I still can't log on. Can you please help me with my password?"

She tapped her nails on her desk while watching the movers haul a stack of chairs from one side of her lab to the other. In her ear, the IT guy made soothing noises while he typed on his own keyboard.

"I'm sorry, Doctor Rose, but your credentials do not appear in the Generation Med system."

"I'm sorry?"

"Your credentials..."

"I heard you the first time." Fear, cold and sinister, churned her stomach. "What about my files?"

She waited, her fingers now tapping her desk faster than before.

"I'm sorry, ma'am, but whatever files you had would have been deleted along with your credentials."

All of her research, all her hard work...she had to keep trying. "What about the backups? You do back up the entire Generation Med system every night, correct?"

"One moment."

Dani didn't wait. Balancing the landline on her shoulder, she pulled out her cell phone and texted Nik: *Trouble. Locked out of Gen Med system. All work lost. Can you call?*

A second passed, then three, then six. It took almost two minutes, then: *Sorry. Bank robbery. Needed. Will call asap.*

Dani switched the handset from one ear to the next just as IT responded.

"I'm sorry, Doctor Rose, but we have nothing in our back up system under your credentials either."

Dani hung up. Fury burned through her. Incompetence. Just plain old fashioned incompetence. She'd have to file a complaint through the Generation Med hierarchy, but she was reluctant to start pushing buttons when they'd been so gracious with her not ten minutes ago.

In reality, she hadn't lost much. The backbone of her

work consisted of the research she'd conducted at Star Haven University. She'd copied those files and erased it from their system even though the University owned her work. Her ex-fiancé wouldn't dare say anything. If he started an investigation of her theft, he'd have to admit he'd been working with, and sleeping with, an Alt. Associating with an Alt in Star Haven was a career killer, the same one that had driven Dani back to Thunder City in the first place.

After she'd uploaded the files from Star Haven University to Generation Med, she'd placed the external drive in a safety deposit box at her new...*oh, shit.*

She pulled out her phone again and clicked on the news app. Streaming headlines spilled across the screen. *Bank robbery in progress at Thunder City Bank & Trust.*

Dani clicked on the headline. A coincidence. It had to be. There's no way it could be her branch.

The headline opened to a news feed. A reporter shouted into her microphone as T-CASS converged on the bank, her bank, right alongside the police. Gunshots could be heard in the background.

Nik. Dani forgot about her research at the thought of Nik phasing into all of that chaos. He'd already been shot once this year. Abilities or not, Alts could get hurt and they could die.

Dani ran out of the lab.

~★~

Ghost rose through the asphalt of Mystic Bay Boulevard two blocks from the bank, where the dispatchers at the Arena had directed him. They had reported an incendiary device had exploded in the middle of the street. Cars swerved, causing accidents. Then, the bank's silent alarms hit the security company monitoring them. The Thunder City police department already had traffic under control, with police detouring commuters down side streets. Fire and Rescue waited their turn nearby. Around him, T-CASS clustered together, in uniform and ready for action.

Captain Spectacular swooped in from the skies, landing light as a feather in the middle of the group, Thomas secure in her arms. Highlight landed right behind her, carrying three trainees on her light slide.

"Mach Ten, make sure the buildings in the surrounding area are clear up to the fourth floors. If not, get the stragglers higher up. Any medical emergencies should be taken to the roof. Rumble and Roar will fly them to Harbor Regional."

Mach Ten sped away, a bright green blur.

"Where's Seeker?" Captain Spectacular called.

"Right here, Captain." Seeker pushed his way forward through the crowd.

"Ghost, get him closer to the bank. Phase him into the car dealership right across the street. Report back what you can see."

Ghost reached out to Seeker. "Ready?"

"Didn't we just leave this party?" Seeker referred to Ghost phasing the pale young man away from the quarry before a mutated Alt could squish him dead the week before.

"The fun never ends." Ghost phased himself and Seeker into the ground. When they reemerged, the car dealership was empty. Mach Ten had already been there and cleared out the showroom floor.

Ghost guided Seeker behind the latest luxury sedan. Huge, showy, with a thick body between Seeker and any stray bullets. "Can you see from here? Do you need a better angle?"

"Let me look around first. I'll let you know." Seeker took off his opaque glasses and faced the general direction of the bank. To an outsider it appeared as if Seeker was staring at the car door. In reality, he pushed his vision through solid layers until he could see through the walls of the dealership and the bank. He didn't have normal human eyes, but an all-black ichor where his eyes should be.

Nik waited, his comm unit relaying new orders to other T-CASS members in his ear.

"There are hostages." Seeker's voice was low, though it really wasn't necessary. "At least twenty-four. They're all in front, near the doors, except one who's in the hallway leading to the back offices. They're already tied up."

Nik handed Seeker his tablet, to which Thomas had pushed a blueprint of the ground floor of the bank. Seeker slipped his glasses back on and started marking the coordinates of the hostages. Then he handed the tablet back to Nik, who transmitted the information to Thomas, who in turn pushed the information to the rest of T-CASS. Nik was proud of Seeker. For a recent graduate to full-time T-CASS member, he'd proven himself quite capable here, and during the quarry raid.

"Highlight," Captain Spec said in Nik's ear. "You get Stampede, Flame, Blockhead, Spritz, and Division Six up to the fourth floor. Make your way down to the first and wait for my signal."

Division Six was the Thunder City SWAT team that worked in tandem with T-CASS. They trained together specifically to make sure neither T-CASS nor the TC police were caught off guard by Norms who thought they could outwit T-CASS or by Chaos Alts who liked to use Norms and T-CASS for target practice.

"Ghost, you grab the hostage in the hallway. Get him out first," Captain Spec continued. "You'll have one minute to grab him, then Highlight will blow open the back door. She'll head to the front doors while Spritz and Blockhead disarm the robbers. Stampede, you cover Flame while she burns the ties off the hostages."

"Wait," Seeker interrupted. "There's something happening in back. There's two men in the safety deposit vault. There're drilling one of the boxes."

"Division Six will handle them. Hostages first, then the vault. Whatever is in there isn't half as important as keeping people alive." The Captain had taken no small amount of heat since the quarry raid and she knew she needed to make up for the loss of life there.

Ghost shifted his stance. He couldn't phase yet. Once he phased into the ground, he couldn't communicate through his comm unit. He spared a brief thought for Dani. Was she following the news? Did she wonder if he was okay? He hoped not. He hoped she was sitting in her office, typing away on her computer, secure in the knowledge that he could take care of himself. He wanted her safe and happy and not thinking of him the way he'd thought of her when she held Fagin at gunpoint.

"They're waiting for something," Seeker said. "They're not taking money from behind the counter. There's no activity except for the drilling in the vault. It's weird."

Ghost agreed. Weird, but the Captain was right. They'd worry about why after the hostages were safe.

"Team One in place," Highlight said.

"Get ready."

Ghost tensed. Seeker glanced over his shoulder. "Good luck."

Ghost nodded. Captain Spec gave her signal and Ghost dropped into the ground.

It only took seconds for him to travel under the road into the walls of the bank and find his way to the corridor. The hostage sat tense and curled in a ball, his head tucked into his knees, just inside the doorway leading away from the main lobby. Three men stood over him with guns. The easiest way out was through the floor.

Ghost gathered himself into a corner. Once he positioned himself directly under the hostage he would bring his hands up around the man's lap, haul him into the ground and hurry back over to the car dealership. It was the fastest route out of here. Once he'd assessed the hostage's situation and checked to see if he was hurt, then Nik would take him to the staging area where the paramedics would take over.

The hostage looked up for a brief second to mutter something to one of the robbers. From this angle Ghost could get a better look at the hostage's face. The man looked familiar — a rough, worn face framed with dark sideburns, with a shot of salt and pepper hair. Ghost quick-checked his memory. He couldn't come up with a name.

A shout from the lobby startled both the robbers and the hostage. Captain Spec must have given Highlight her signal. There was a boom and a rush of noise. The robbers pulled their guns closer, triggers ready. Ghost hoped the hostage didn't try to run.

Ghost slithered under the feet of the robbers and made his grab. He expected a shout or a shove or some sort of resistance from the hostage — they all reacted that way when he unexpectedly pulled them into a wall or floor. Even Dani had shivered in his arms the first time, tensing up. It was an automatic reaction that couldn't be helped.

Nothing happened with this guy. It took Ghost a second to realize that he'd missed. He didn't have the hostage. Shit! Now the robbers would be alerted to his presence.

Ghost made another grab. Nothing again. Something was preventing him from bringing the hostage into his world. From inside the floor, he couldn't contact the Captain to request backup. He had to unphase to stop the robbers from murdering the hostage. He had no choice. He spared a brief thought for Dani, lying in his arms, her sweet breath tickling his ear, her desire riding him hard.

He wanted her in his life forever. If he survived this he would propose to her. But he had to succeed first.

Ghost rose through the floor putting his body between the guns and the hostage. "Don't shoot!"

He circled the hostage, so all three robbers could see his arms raised. "Don't shoot. Let him go. I'll stay."

The three robbers didn't move any closer, but their weapons were aimed at his head.

"Oh, you're not staying, Ghost. You're leaving. With us."

It wasn't one of the robbers who spoke. Ghost looked down at the hostage. A spark of electricity crackled in the man's hands as he stood. The crackle turned louder as the spark turned into a ball of raw power.

Ghost stepped back to avoid the hostage's swipe. He'd been set up, but by whom? Why? One of the robbers shoved him toward the "hostage". Ghost took a closer look at the man's face. He could see the resemblance now. There had only been one other electricity manipulator in Thunder City and Cory had killed him before the quarry raid.

"Now do you know who I am? Your brother killed my son. The Blackwoods are going to pay for that."

Ghost crouched to fight, but it was too late. The gun behind him pushed him right into the electricity ball. His body exploded with pain and he fell to the floor, unconscious.

CHAPTER EIGHT

Dani turned down a side street and parked her car when it became obvious traffic was going nowhere fast. Thank heavens she'd decided to give her feet a break and had worn flats with her slacks instead of heels. The flats made it easier for her to run the half mile with the back pack she pulled from her trunk. She jogged toward the street corner where the flashing blue lights of the police mixed with the flashing red of the fire and rescue vehicles. She'd only made it to within twenty yards or so when a huge man with a huge gun stopped her in her tracks.

"I'm sorry, ma'am. You can't go any further."

Dani couldn't dance this dance with Nik's life on the line, so she ditched subtlety. "I need to speak to Hack-Man." She used Carraro's moniker to make it clear who she was talking about. "My name is Doctor Daniella Rose. I have information he needs. This isn't a bank robbery, it's a kidnapping. Ghost is the target. You can't send him in there. You have to stop this operation."

The cop looked doubtful, but he relayed her information anyway. A minute passed. Then another. Dani paced a few feet, left to right, looking for someplace where she could shift without drawing attention. Wicked and vain poked its evil into her head. She'd fight her way to Carraro if she had to, damn the consequences.

Another man approached. He had short-clipped black hair, east Asian eyes, and was wearing a blue polo shirt with black pants. "It's okay. I'll bring her."

The cop let her pass. The blue-shirted man directed her toward a van sitting on the edge of the activity. He slid the door open and offered her a hand as she stepped up into what looked a like a command center.

"Thank you, Shinzo."

Carraro didn't even turn around in his seat to look at her. She'd never met him in person and had only communicated with him via email. He'd sent a message once to confirm her order and once again after installation. He had far more important clients than her. The setup inside the van had him tracking every Alt and every cop, inside and outside of the bank.

"If you have something to say, say it. The operation has already started. We can't abort now." Carraro still didn't look at her, his eyes following the half dozen screens surrounding him.

"This isn't a bank robbery. It's a set-up," Dani repeated. "There's a drug lord, Fredek Varga — "

"Fagin," Carraro said, his eyes still on the computer screens.

Good. He knew who she was talking about so she didn't have to waste time explaining. "He wiped out my credentials at Generation Med after he erased all of my research, including the back-ups. My personal back-up to my research, my original research, is in a safety deposit box at this bank. Fagin wants to destroy my back-up and use Nik to get to me. He has to stop my research before it stops him from re-creating his network. In order to shut me down, he has to kill me."

This garnered her a glance, nothing more. "And, what exactly are you researching that would capture the attention of Fagin?"

"A cure for blitz addiction. Permanent. It would put him out of business if everyone used it."

Carraro raised his hand to shut her up. "Repeat again, Seeker? Someone else has entered the vault?"

She watched as Carraro hit a button. This time Seeker's voice echoed through the van. "There's a third man in the safety deposit vault. They've stopped drilling. Whatever it is they wanted, they have it."

"My external hard drive." She was too late to save the drive, but. . . "Let them have it. All I care about is Nik."

This time Carraro gave her more a more thorough look. Any fears she had about being wrong, about this being a mistake, melted. Her instincts had hit the mark. Carraro knew it, but the operation was already in play. Carraro leaned toward a mic. "Captain, we have a problem. Listen in: Seeker, can you see Ghost?"

There was a short pause. "No, should I? I figured he'd pull the hostage from under the flooring."

"Do you see the hostage? Is he still there?" Carraro asked.

"Yes, sir. I see him."

"Keep an eye on the hostage. When he disappears, let me know immediately."

"Yes, sir."

"Captain?" Carraro addressed his wife. "This may be a set-up to kidnap Ghost. We need to focus our efforts on the hostage in the hallway and the three men in the vault. The rest is a distraction."

He was quick, Dani thought. He'd figured out

Fagin's tactic before she had to explain. Fagin would have hired local guns from the pool of wannabe gang bangers looking to prove themselves. He would give them enough information to make the plan sellable to the not-so-bright, then let them take the fall while he made his escape.

"Ghost is down!" Seeker's voice shouted. "He unphased, then the hostage knocked him out. The hostage Ghost tried to protect is working for the robbers."

"Shots fired in the lobby!" someone else shouted. Dani didn't know who. She watched the activity as it unfolded on the screens.

"Get the hostages out there. We'll figure out who's working for who later." This from Captain Spec.

Sparks flashed across the screens. Fire ripped across the lobby followed by a bright beam of light. The robbers tried to fight T-CASS, but T-CASS had the co-ordination and determination needed to win. Fagin's men quickly found themselves surrounded and disarmed.

What about Nik?

"Captain, Ghost is gone. With all the activity in the lobby I couldn't see what happened. He's not in the hallway. I don't know if he phased into the floor again. I can't see the hostage either," Seeker said.

Dani clenched her fists. She had to speak up. "What about the vault?"

"Division Six, report?" Carraro called.

"This is D6. We got the two drillers. They're down." Carraro looked back at her.

"Do they have the external hard drive?"

Carraro asked the question. D6 called back. "No, sir. There's nothing on them. No jewels, no papers, no tech, nothing."

"Fagin was the third man in the vault," she said, heartsick. "They passed the drive off to him during the commotion in the lobby. He left them there to get caught."

Carraro turned away from the computers, his hand stretched out to her. "We'll find Nik. We'll get him back alive."

Dani turned away. The door to van slid open under her touch. No, there was no *we* in this operation. By the time T-CASS had organized itself, she would know where Fagin had taken Nik and she'd get him back on her own. After she killed Fagin.

~★~

By now the teen thug who had tailed her last night would have reported to Fagin that Dodger was back in town. The fact that Fagin had launched a bank robbery and didn't take any money meant one of two things: either he had a larger source of cash from somewhere to rebuild his network, or he was counting on catching Dodger and forcing Dodger to give back the money he'd stolen.

If the former was true, then Dani had to hope that Fagin wanted vengeance on Dodger more than he wanted the money. It was the only way to find Fagin, and Nik, faster than T-CASS: Let Fagin catch Dodger and pray Fagin didn't kill him in cold blood before he could kill Fagin.

Dani shifted to Daniel and returned to the Mystic Bay Health Recovery Center. He had no gun this time, no cell phone, and no plan beyond making himself a target. Daniel looked like an easy capture, but not too easy. Fagin was single minded, not stupid. Daniel couldn't let Fagin think he was working undercover for T-CASS.

The catch was that he couldn't afford to let Fagin knock Daniel unconscious. Doing so could result in Daniel shifting to Daniella while knocked out and giving away his only advantage. He had to take the fight to Fagin, find Nik, and escape. Shouldn't be too much of a problem for old vain and wicked.

Daniel leaned against the wall at the mouth of the alley, his shoulders scrunched down to hide his height, for well over an hour. Addicts enrolled in the center's outpatient program came and went by bus and taxi, ignoring him as best they could. They knew why he was there. Two of the security guards even tried to get him to move on, but Daniel made it clear he wasn't doing anything illegal and wouldn't be moving any time soon.

The sun had just started to set when he spotted Fagin's goons turning the corner around the gas station. He recognized two of them from the parking lot holdup, still dressed in black saggy jeans and hoodies. Good. He already knew their weaknesses. The only way this hair-brained scheme would work was if he could convince them to take Dodger without too much fighting.

The boys spotted him. Head up, balls out. Dani had never felt so far away.

"Hey, you!"

Daniel ducked his head back down to examine his fingernails, scraping off what was left of Dani's nail polish. He didn't bother acknowledging the goons until they were in his face.

"I'm talking to you," the smaller one said, spittle flying as he shoved himself into Daniel's personal space. He was almost as tall as Daniel, but not nearly as wide. The larger one had the width but not the height. The three behind them fell in between.

"These do work, kid." Daniel pointed to his ears.

"Fagin wants a word with you."

Daniel laughed. "Oh, I think Fagin wants a lot more than to talk to me. He didn't tell you what I did to him ten years ago, did he?"

The kid backed off. "Yeah, he told us. You betrayed him. Stole his money. He wants it back."

"That's it?" Now that Daniel had drawn the goons in close, it was time to pour on the intimidation. Daniel pushed himself off the wall. Daniel was six foot two, but with an extra push Daniel could hit Dodger's six foot seven in five seconds. The kid just figured out how big Dodger could be when he wanted to show off everything. "He didn't tell you the rest?"

The other four started to spread out, covering their bases, looking worried.

"He told us," the kid said, trying not to lose his bravado. "He told us everything. He told us how you started the blitz wars. He told us how you sent three of his best distributors into ambushes you set up with 'Low Down' Lazar Malloy. Then, you gave almost all of Fagin's stash from the shipyards to the Left Fists in Star Haven. Then, after Fagin got busted, you raided his accounts and stole all of his money. The man couldn't even pay for his own lawyer. Ended up in jail for ten years."

The evil of Dodger's acts from ten years ago shamed Daniel now, but he couldn't let the wannabes see it. Instead, he treated them to a small smirk. "It was just a little lovers' spat. Someday, I'll tell you what I do to people who really piss me off."

The wannabes jerked back at the phrase *lovers' spat.* Dodger did his best to look shocked. "What? Fagin didn't tell you I was his boyfriend? That's the most interesting part of this tale."

"Fagin ain't no homo." Wannabe number one backed up just little more.

"Oh, you don't think so?" Daniel sighed. "The stories I could tell you. I mean, Fagin may be nothing to look at, but in bed..."

"Shut UP!"

Now he had the wannabes confused. On one hand, Fagin had probably promised them the wealth of the city treasury to bring in Dodger, but the idea that they were working for a faggot probably didn't sit too well with them either.

"Well, boys. This has been fun, but I have clients I need to see. So, why don't all of you take a walk and I'll forget we had this conversation." Daniel made a "shoo, fly" motion with his hands.

That's all it took to get the fists flying. Daniel played with them for a while, knocked one out clean cold and drop-kicked another into the nearest lamp post. The crunch of bone against metal sent a shriek across the din of traffic. No one in the cars that passed by bothered to do anything to break up the fight. At one point, the two security guards returned. Daniel let one of the boys' fists connect so he could stagger back toward the guards. He grabbed one guard by the neck and told them both to run if they knew what was good for them. The guards ran back into the Center. They didn't get paid enough to deal with someone like Daniel when he was Dodger-sized.

Still, it was time to bring this to a close. Daniel waited until the kid pulled out his gun and aimed it at Daniel. Daniel yanked the nearest wannabe in front of him, so the wannabe got hit in the arm by the bullet.

Even the horror at shooting someone other than his target didn't break through the kid's anger. He raised the gun again, but Daniel knew not to push his luck. Sirens blared in the background. The wannabe with the bullet and the other one with the broken bones would live — if they kept their mouths shut.

"All right." Daniel raised his hands in the air and got down on his knees. "I'm done. I'd rather go with you than the cops."

"Get up." The kid waved the gun at Daniel. From the gas station, a black van rolled over the curb and opened a door. "Get in."

Daniel got in. The kid kept the gun at Daniel's head while yelling at the driver. "Get us out of here. The cops are coming."

The wheels of the van squealed as it roared away from the corner.

Just a little bit longer and Daniel would fix what Dodger had broken. He'd fix his past and his future and bring Nik home alive.

CHAPTER NINE

Nik woke to a light show and a headache. He turned his head a little, not bothering to hide a grimace. The light show flashed even faster, and a whip-thin strand of electricity lashed out and whacked his ear. The pain raced across his forehead.

"Doesn't feel good, does it?"

Nik remembered the voice. Shocker, Electrocyte's father. Father and son had been transplants from Star Haven. Both had wanted to return to the city that had kicked out all of the Alts. They had joined the protesters at the harbor when the ferry service refused to sell them tickets. Electrocyte had taken the ferry company's president hostage. Nik had been on the ferry, had tried to stop Electrocyte from killing the president. Instead, both of them had been shot by Cory. Electrocyte died at the scene. Nik had survived, only because Hannah Quinn had used her power to save his life.

No wonder his ability had failed him. Shocker, like his son, could manipulate electricity. Nik couldn't phase through anything not solid like water — or electricity. Shocker must have used his power to surround himself with electrical current so Nik couldn't grab him. Now he held Nik suspended horizontally off the ground at a height of about six feet, surrounded by an electrical cocoon. Nik was stuck until Shocker turned off the current, which he didn't seemed inclined to do.

"Shocker, I'm sorry..."

"Save it, I'm not interested in your words."

So much for talking him out of revenge. "It won't work, Shocker. They'll figure out that you're after Cory. They'll figure out you're using me to do it. They won't let Cory come here alone." Wherever here was.

"It doesn't matter. I have you. That's enough. Alive or dead, your family is going to suffer."

Negotiating skills didn't run in Shocker's side of the family, so how would he have put together a gang of men willing to walk into a fake bank robbery? Nik tried to wiggle around in his cocoon, but only got more shocks on his face for the effort. At least he still wore his uniform. It kept the rest of his body insulated from Shocker's damage. For the first time in his life, though, he wished he wore a mask to protect his face. Looking at the ceiling, he could see what looked like metal and rivets, but it was too low to be the ceiling in one of Fagin's old warehouses.

Pathia? He called to the T-CASS telepath. No response. She might not be able to hear him through the noise of the cocoon. He was on his own.

Nik was racing through a list of possible locations with low, metal ceilings when a door to his right opened. The sound distracted Shocker long enough to allow Nik to turn his head without getting a shock. Two of Fagin's men tossed a much larger man into the room before backing out and locking the door behind them. The new guy's hands were tied behind his back. He stared at Nik, allowing Nik a good look at the man's face.

Setting aside height and build, Nik focused on the

face. High cheekbones, an almost sweet baby-face, with swept-back brown hair pulled into a...*fucking hell*. It was Dodger. Fagin's right-hand man who wore a man-bun long before it came into fashion. Nik had only ever seen one picture of him, but it had been enough. His rage jerked his body closer to the electrical barrier, but he ignored the pain. He would bring Dodger to justice if it was the last thing he did.

Dodger for his part either didn't recognize Ghost, or didn't care. He walked over to Shocker and leaned on the back wall next to him.

"So, what's your story?"

Before Shocker could answer, the door opened again. Fagin. Three others joined him.

"Why isn't he tied up?" Fagin motioned to the three behind him.

Dodger looked surprised and turned to show off his hands behind his back. "I am tied up."

"Knees and ankles," Fagin ordered.

Dodger let loose an exaggerated moan. "There was a time when you would have tied me up yourself. And, you would have enjoyed it more."

Nik couldn't believe what he heard. Dodger and Fagin, a couple? Something for him to file away for after he captured them both. He just needed to find a way around the cocoon. The problem was that phasing through solid matter was just a question of squeezing in between the stationary molecules, but when he was phasing through liquids or electricity, he had to weave his way between moving molecules. When the rate of speed of one part of his body exceeded the rate of speed of another part of his body, it cause a great deal of pain, and he risked unphasing without all of his body parts located where they belonged. It was dangerous, but getting out of here before Fagin pulled Dani into his trap was worth the risk. He just needed to get close enough to the cocoon without Shocker noticing.

When Dodger distracted Shocker, Nik had swung closer to the electrical border. Now he needed Dodger to distract Shocker again.

"You see him?" Fagin pointed to Nik. The last thing he needed was more attention. "You're next unless you tell me what you did with my money."

"I don't have your money. I spent it all. Why do you think I'm still selling on street corners?"

It took all three of Fagin's men to hold Dodger still so Fagin could backhand him. Nik wasn't sorry to see that; but he only wished he was the one who had done it. "If that's true, then you're going to die up there."

Dodger spat blood on Fagin's shoes. "Kidnapping a Blackwood? Not cool, Fagin. If you kill him, the non-lethal force agreement Cap Spec made with the city might not apply."

"First, they have to find him," Fagin said, arms akimbo. "Which they won't. Then, they'll have to find his body. Which they won't. And then, they'll have to prove I did it. Which they won't, because I'm not the one who's going to do it. Right, Shocker?"

Shocker shrugged. "Whatever you say, boss."

Fagin looked down at Dodger, now tied at the ankles and knees. "You see. You give a man what he wants more than anything else in the world and he'll be loyal for life."

"Until you betray him." Dodger threw off the men who'd tied him up. "I'd've been loyal if you had just taken the time to bail me out of jail instead of replacing me in your bed."

Fagin grunted once, checked the Dodger's ropes,

then he slammed out of the door, his henchmen close behind. Dodger waited a beat, then rolled his body — head over ankles — under Nik's cocoon until he sat next to Shocker. Shocker for his part pulled one hand away from maintaining Nik's cocoon. Nik drifted down. *Just a little bit further. A little bit further.*

"Ouch!" Dodger jumped back. "What was that for?"

Shocker must have hit Dodger with an electrical shock. "I'm not untying you so don't ask. If you try to distract me from killing Nik Blackwood, I'll just kill him more slowly."

"Fine, then." Dodger scooted further away from Shocker — but not that much further — and pouted.

Damn. Nik needed Dodger to fight Shocker before Fagin showed up again. It was back on him to talk Shocker out of siding with Fagin.

"Shocker, listen to me. If Fagin could betray someone like Dodger — someone who gave everything he had to Fagin — what makes you think Fagin won't kill you, once you kill me?"

"Doesn't matter. Without my son, it doesn't matter."

Oh, great. A murderer with a suicide bid.

"Hey, Shocker?"

This from Dodger. Nik could only see what happened next out of the corner of his eye. Dodger had somehow worked his ropes loose. He rammed his whole body into Shocker. There wasn't even a scuffle. Dodger knocked out Shocker clean and cold.

Nik fell as a dead weight. Only years of practice allowed him to phase before he hit the floor, saving himself a broken back and a cracked skull.

He waited in the flooring until he got his wits about him. Shocker still breathed, but his head wouldn't heal anytime soon. Dodger...what did Dodger think he was doing? The over-muscled son-of-a-bitch discarded the remnants of the rope used to tie him up. He walked to the center of the room and sat cross legged, his arms raised in the air.

"Nik. I know you're still here. I can see the floor breathe. I freed you. You owe me. Come on out and let's talk."

Nik hesitated. He'd never fought Dodger. He'd never gotten close. No one had. Dodger might have height and weight on his side, but what about skills? Nik had a couple of blackbelts in various martial arts, but what did Dodger have?

"Nik, please. I won't hurt you, I promise. I'm not the same person I was ten years ago. My name is Daniel, not Dodger. I've been an upstanding citizen for quite some time now. I came here because I don't want to see Fagin hurt you or anyone else."

If Dodger was lying, Nik was still at a disadvantage. The electricity Shocker had sent through him did damage. He might not have the energy to fight back.

"Nik. I know what your priorities are. You want to save Daniella Rose. Believe it or not, I want to save Dani, too. I know her. She would want you to talk to me. You might be able to sneak out of here, go around Fagin and his men, but they'll be gone before you can call in T-CASS to help you. You can't take them on by yourself. Together, you and I can stop them. You and I can bring down Fagin once and for all. I know it means trusting me, and trusting me is the last thing in the world you want to do, but please. Just talk to me, man to man, and you'll see — I'm not that different from you."

Dodger knew Dani? How? Why? Wait, he knew why. Dodger must have been the dealer at the frat party where Dani had been arrested. It was the only explanation that made sense.

And yet, the pretty words from Dodger's bass voice made Nik want to believe that Dodger really did want to help Dani. Nik had to believe because at the end of it all, Dodger was right. Nik couldn't fight all of Fagin's thugs by himself, and Fagin would disappear before Nik could escape and call for help.

Nik unphased at the far corner of the room. He nearly collapsed, too. His body twitched like a blitz junky. Blood poured from his nose.

"All right," Nik wiped the blood away with his sleeve. "Talk to me. Why should I trust you?"

"My name is Daniel. You know me. You don't think you do, but you do. I would never hurt you, Nik. Not even when we were in high school. Not even when I was doing awful things, I would never have done anything to put you in danger."

"Like selling me blitz?" Nik didn't hold back his outrage. "Getting me hooked on the stuff and then withholding it if I couldn't pay?"

"Yes," Dodger agreed. "Like selling you blitz."

"Do you have any idea of the damage you inflicted?" He couldn't understand. There was no way a guy like Dodger could know what he did to the people Nik cared about.

"Yes, Nik. I know the damage. I saw the results of what I did while I was in jail."

"When were you arrested?" Nik double-checked his memory. "I would have known if you'd been busted."

"It's complicated."

"Maybe for you. Not for the rest of us." Nik spat through blood-covered lips. "You never saw Molly Cathers."

"I remember Molly. I saw her right before she OD'd. We shared a holding cell together before her arraignment. She's one of the reasons why I changed."

Nik snorted. "She was a child."

"So was I!" Dodger scooted closer. Nik didn't back away, but he didn't step forward either. "You and I are almost the same age. We went to the same schools. We knew the same kids. We were in class together."

Dodger was delusional. "I don't know you."

"Yes, you do!" Dodger crept even closer. "Look me in the eyes and tell me you don't know me."

Nik backed up to the nearest wall. A trick. This was all a trick. Dodger was too big, too menacing. He'd have remembered someone that huge from school.

"C'mon, Nik. I'm not going to hurt you. If I'd wanted to, I'd have done it by now. Look me in the eyes and tell me you don't know me."

Dodger returned back to the middle of the room, giving Nik room to move, space to think. There was a single fluorescent light over his head. Now, with Shocker unconscious, it was the only light they had.

Never let it be said that Nik Blackwood was a coward. He walked over to Dodger, who got onto his knees, held his head back, and let the light shine into his eyes.

They were lavender. Nik only knew one person with lavender eyes. Not even Dani's brother, Robby, had eyes that color.

"I know what you're thinking, Nik. You're right. I'm a shifter. An Alt, just like you."

With that Dodger started to shrink, his face turned softer, rounder, his clothes bunching up around his body.

"I've been able to change genders since I was eight. I never told anyone, not even my parents. If anyone had known they would have stopped Robby's first transplant. My parents would have hated me even more. I let the transplants continue, not understanding the medical implications."

There she was. Daniella, sitting before him in a pool of oversized clothing. Her voice was as light and airy as he remembered.

"I meant what I said, Nik. I was a child, too. I wouldn't have hurt anyone if I had truly understood the consequences of what I was doing. You've met my parents. You've seen how Robby acts. Don't tell me you don't know how they treated me."

She was begging for his forgiveness. Seeing her sitting there as Dani, he wanted to grant it, but he still had a lot of old anger inside him. She reached out to touch his face, but he pulled back before she could reach him.

His head wanted to abandon her, but his heart wanted to forgive her. He was trapped between both in a snare of his own making.

~★~

"Let's get out of here," Nik said.

Dani pulled back. Tacit approval or just a temporary truce? She'd settle for a truce. Now wasn't the time to push her luck. "One minute."

She shifted back, while Nik watched her with an eagle eye. Shifters weren't unheard of in T-CASS or in the Alt community at large. Dani had checked over the years. From what she knew, though, most shifters had only one shift, but it was tied to another ability. Blockhead was a good example — his hands became unbreakable blocks, but he also had strength beyond normal men. Nowhere had she found information on someone who shifted their entire gender.

No matter. Only for Nik — Ghost — would she

change her form in front of anyone. She pushed her shift beyond Daniel's size. For this, they'd need Dodger. If nothing else, he was intimidating as hell. Fagin knew it but the rest of his untrained crew would learn the hard way.

"Do you know where we are?" Ghost asked as she swept her hair back up into a bun.

"Sinclair Ships's graveyard," Dodger's voice answered. "On one of the old-styled ferries that was decommissioned before the new hydrofoils replaced them. We're in what would have been a storage room for the commissary."

Dodger stood up to face Ghost, who looked back at Dodger like a strange bug. "You don't need to figure me out yet. I just need you to watch my back."

"Are you any good in a fight?"

"Better than you." He couldn't help it. He winked at Ghost just as the door creaked open. Dodger turned, keeping his body between the door and Ghost. "Stay behind me."

"No, wait."

There was no waiting. Fagin's crew poured in ahead of Fagin. Dodger didn't hesitate. He used surprise to his advantage and tore through them with a viciousness he hadn't let loose since high school. He didn't kill. He refused to go that far, but he broke multiple bones in every single one of Fagin's crew. There was even an Alt or three hiding in the group. One tried to put the whammy on him with spikes from his knuckles. Those hurt. One of the spikes pierced Dodger's clothes, but missed piercing his upper shoulder by a millimeter. It didn't slow Dodger down in the slightest. Instead, Dodger used the pain as motivation to push through a series of moves that left the Alt pinned to the floor by his own spikes with both of his eyes blackened and his nose broken.

Ghost didn't try to stop him during the fight, and even assisted where needed. Ghost hadn't lied — he had the moves. With half of Fagin's men unconscious and bleeding, they headed into the corridor. Fagin had abandoned his men as soon as the fight broke out, as Dodger had expected.

"Which way?" Nik asked.

Dodger pointed toward the stern. "The deck is still intact."

Dodger paused once or twice to make sure Ghost kept up, but Ghost pushed through the pain. He hopped in and out of the walls and floors, giving Dodger a rundown of how many men were ahead of them, even putting down two of Fagin's crew on his own. Dodger let him. Sometimes a guy needed a good fight just to prove he could still do it. Ghost's nosebleed continued to worry Dodger, though, but Ghost didn't complain.

Dodger collected a fair share of guns along the way. He offered one to Ghost. Ghost hesitated, the temptation obvious, but he refused. Fagin would be armed. They both knew it, but Ghost wouldn't break the oath he made to Thunder City. In turn, Dodger wouldn't be able to fire first and put an end to Fagin. Not with Ghost present. He had to play this by Ghost's rules or he — or rather Dani — would lose him forever. Dodger still hoped Nik wouldn't abandon Dani. Dani wasn't so sure.

"He can't have much more in the way of crew. He has no money," Ghost said, out of breath from the last fight.

Hang in there, Ghost. It's almost over. "I suspect he's got some outside funding source. Not sure from where.

His crew is lean, but he's paying them from somewhere and it's not from blitz distribution. Fagin can sweet talk a good deal out of people, but no one works for free. Not even for him."

Ghost scouted ahead one last time. "He's up on the sun deck. He's got binocs on the Bay. He's waiting on something, or someone."

"How many crew?" Dodger was getting tired. Ghost had to be exhausted.

"Four. Three near the door, one next to him."

"Alts?" The previous ones had caught them off guard.

"No one I recognize, but if he's working with unregistered Alts, who knows." Ghost gave a half-hearted shrug. Poor guy was done. Fagin wouldn't have fed him before Shocker imprisoned him in his web of torture. All that pain could drain a man faster than a hard workout.

"You stay here," Dodger said. "I'll take care of this."

"No." Ghost put a hand on Dodger's shoulder. Dodger froze, not wanting to draw Ghost's attention to the contact. Not wanting to break the moment. "I'll phase into the floor of the deck. I can pull two at time through the floor. If I get them down far enough, I can just leave them there. By the time they run up here, I'll be back to help you, and we'll have taken down the other two and Fagin."

"And, if they're Alts?" Dodger asked. "If they can somehow get up here faster? Or hurt you so you can't get back up here?"

"I can play hide and seek with the best of them. Slow them up. I have skills beyond phasing." Ghost sounded offended. "I'll know what to expect this time."

"All right, then. Let's do this. On the count of three. One...two..."

Nik phased into the wall.

"...Three." Dodger shook his head and waited for the shouts of outrage. He didn't have to wait long. The third crew member charged down the stairs and right into Dodger's fist. Dodger tossed him over the rail and onto the floor below.

On deck, the fourth crew member didn't hesitate to pull his gun, but Dodger already had a borrowed Sig, ready to fire. He killed the crew member. Ghost would understand the need for self-defense. Fagin just stood there with his back to Dodger. His former right hand man and lover.

"Go ahead and shoot, if you want." Fagin put the binoculars down.

"You know I won't. I'm not the man you raised me to be anymore."

"Is that what I did? Raise you?" Fagin did turn around now. If he was afraid of being shot he didn't show it.

"You gave me confidence." Dodger kept his gun ready, just in case. "You gave me praise. You gave me skills. You gave me affection."

"And for that, you'll shoot me?" Fagin snarled. "If I did so much for you, then tell me what you did with my money and walk away. I won't come after you. I just need that money."

He must have borrowed the money to start this operation and now the lenders wanted their money back. The lenders must also be on their way. Why else would Fagin still be on board the ferry? "I told you. I don't have the money."

"Yeah, yeah." Fagin turned his back on Dodger again. "You spent it all, you said. I don't believe you."

"You're right. I lied."

Fagin peeked over his shoulder.

"I set up an account and contacted an attorney. She gave the anonymous donation to Catherine Blackwood. A check for 1.2 million dollars with specific instructions to create drug rehab centers across Thunder City."

Fagin choked. "You gave 1.2 million to a billionaire?"

"Catherine Blackwood had no reason to betray me. And, she didn't. Your money has funded a dozen drug rehab centers over the past ten years."

Fagin laughed like a dying man gasping for his last breath. "Well, I guess there's no reason to keep you around, is there?"

Fagin knew he was going to die, either by Dodger or the lenders. Better that than to go to jail. Over Fagin's shoulder Dodger saw a wave of color coming toward the ferry graveyard. Ghost had contacted T-CASS somehow and alerted them to their location. Fagin turned, his gun pulled, but he never got off a shot. Dodger fired and put the bullet exactly where he aimed. Right into Fagin's skull.

Fagin collapsed forward, dead before he hit the deck.

Dodger placed the gun on the deck. Best not to give T-CASS an excuse to attack him.

"It's over."

Ghost. How much had he overheard?

"For Fagin." Dodger nodded as the wave of color drew closer, police helicopters flying right beside them. Captain Spec must have pulled out the stops to bring in the choppers. "What do I do now?"

"There will be questions. Lots of questions."

Dodger looked at Ghost. "Will you stand by me?"

Ghost nodded, no hesitation this time. "I will."

"And, after?" Was it too much to hope that Ghost —

Nik — would stick by Dani, too?

"After...we'll talk."

Talk. It was a start. If not of a new beginning, then of an end to their relationship. At least Dani still had hope.

CHAPTER TEN

Dani pulled another pint of cookies and cream ice cream out of her freezer. Three pints in one day and she was only halfway through her movie marathon. She needed it. She deserved it. She wanted it.

Nik hadn't been kidding about the questions after their respective kidnappings. It had been four days of endless interrogations, examinations, and deliberations. Serena Jakes had tried to get her deported for refusing to shift at the command of the T-CASS Oversight Committee as proof that she had control over her abilities. Dani had never had a beef with Serena during high school. They'd operated in two separate social circles. Yet, Dani knew her bad-girl rep wouldn't die easy for Nik's ex. Which was why Dani demanded Serena recuse herself from the Committee. The outrage on Serena's face would have been funny except old vain and wicked only cared about protecting Dani's dignity, not about gloating over her win at scoring Nik's affection.

But, had she really won? Nik had kept his word and stayed by Dani's side. He made his reports as thorough and to the point as possible. He supported Dani, but not with the over-enthusiasm of a lover.

Dani had held out hope for their relationship until

tonight. The investigation was ongoing, but everyone knew about Daniel and everyone knew about Dodger. There was outrage from former blitz addicts and the families of those who hadn't survived their addiction. She'd expected that. Catherine produced the paperwork verifying what Dani had told the Committee about the stolen money she had donated for the clinics, but it didn't help much. Generation Med offered limited testimony that they had hired her based on her preliminary research into finding a cure for blitz addiction. They didn't give details. That information helped a little bit, but there were still some folks who would never forgive.

Folks like Nik. She knew how to take a hint. He never tried to contact her outside of the official investigation. No flowers, no dinners, no dancing on the dance floor or in his bed.

Now she had nothing. Generation Med still employed her but her job was nothing more than that: a job. Killing Fagin had killed a piece of her, too. A piece that she hated, but had still been a motivating factor in her life. She'd wanted more than anything to make up for what she'd done, for who she'd been. To erase the damage Dodger had brought into so many lives. She'd thought she'd done the right thing by burying whatever dreams she had of doing something else, anything else, and instead dedicating her life to curing blitz addiction. Without motivation, all she wanted to do was sit on her couch in her pretty princess pajamas and fuzzy slippers, eat ice cream, and cry while watching action movies.

Yes, she was crying. Real tears poured down her cheeks, even before the opening credits to the movie rolled.

No motivation and no Nik. She stuffed another scoop of ice cream into her mouth. Even the bliss of sugar tasted bland without Nik.

A shadow fell over her. Dani held her breath but didn't budge. Nik had phased directly into her living room. Nik, not Ghost. He was dressed as casually as she'd ever seen him, in blue jeans and a white oxford shirt. He walked around the couch to stand where she could see him. He said nothing. She was too scared to move, the ice cream dripping down the back of her throat.

He moved a throw pillow from his corner of the couch so he could sit next to her, but still too far away to touch her. He didn't try to comfort her. He just sat with her as the movie rolled across the screen. She didn't talk, even as she finished her ice cream.

The movie ended. The heroes rode off into the sunset. Nik turned to her, but she couldn't face him.

"I miss you." He leaned forward, caught a curl of hair in his fingers and tucked it behind her ear.

"I miss you, too." She kept her eyes on the screen as the end credits rolled. Her stomach cramped, rebelling against what she needed to say. "But, I don't miss you so much that I'm going to let you back into my life unless you can love me. All of me."

She clutched the ice cream carton closer, her fingers crushing the cardboard, and waited, still watching the screen.

"Dodger is a hard act to get over." Nik reached for the remote and shut off the TV. She had to face him now.

"Dodger was just that. An act," she said. "I'm not that monster. Not anymore. I haven't been for over ten years. I've said my apologies. I've given my testimony.

I'm not going to spend my life, however long that may be, defending what I did as a hurt and angry teenager."

"There's a call by some folks for your arrest." Nik raised his hand at her attempt to protest. "I'm not telling you to threaten you. I'm telling you so you can prepare."

"There's nothing to prepare." Dani twisted in her seat to stab her spoon into the empty carton. "The judge dismissed the charges from my original arrest. Everything else is already past the statute of limitations. There's no evidence for any prosecutor to present. I'm sure as hell not going to put myself in jail just to make others feel better. There's too much work to be done."

Oh. There was her motivation. She knew she'd placed it around here somewhere. All she'd needed was Nik to help her find it again.

Nik nodded. "I know. If it helps any, Thomas sent me over here to tell you he managed to find your research."

"I thought Fagin destroyed it." No one had found the drive anywhere on Fagin or on the ferry.

"He probably did, but Thomas managed to find a copy on a back-up server somewhere. You probably don't want to dig too deep in that direction, either. Just be glad he loves a challenge and he finds you intriguing."

"Nice to know somebody does," Dani muttered.

Nik closed his eyes. "I deserve that. I know I've been distant, but there's a lot to come to grips with and I didn't want to influence the investigation with my bias."

Dani huffed and shoved back against the couch. "That's the problem with you two-shoes. Always doing the right thing for everyone except yourselves."

"Yeah, well — that comes with the territory when

you join T-CASS."

Dani snorted. She couldn't help it. T-CASS wasn't high on her list of favorite organizations right now.

"So, will you?" Nik asked.

"Will I what?" Nik had better not be suggesting what she thought he was suggesting.

"Join T-CASS?»

"Have you been snorting blitz?" Damn the man. What was he thinking? "You know your ex-girlfriend almost got me kicked out of Thunder City because I wouldn't do a strip tease for the Oversight Committee."

"No one is asking you to do a strip tease." Nik ran his hand through his own hair this time. She'd forgotten he did that when he was frustrated. It sent his adorbs score through the roof. Oh, she was back in dangerous territory now. Vain and wicked was in rare form tonight. "Catherine has excused Serena from your review. No one from your past is going to be there. You shift once or twice, with your clothes on, run through a series of exercises, and you're done. It's about proving you have control, nothing else."

"It's not like I have any real power, anyway." Dani knew she could pout with the best of them. "I change my gender. I don't have super strength or anything like that."

"It's still an Alt ability. Blockhead will be there too. He's a shifter. He'll understand."

Dani wasn't so sure about that. Nik was right, though. Not having anyone from her past gawking at her made it a little bit better. Also, according the rules, she wasn't allowed to touch anyone until she could prove she had control. No skin-on-skin contact allowed, according to the Committee. "I guess I'll have to meet with them before my surgery."

Another horror story she had to deal with. The medical community was up in arms that they had unknowingly performed multiple transplants between an Alt and a Norm. On the up side, as the only Norm to have received multiple transplants from an Alt, Robby was more the center of attention than ever before. Would he ever develop Alt power? He was lined up for a long string of tests to see what other changes his body might have undergone, and judging by his television interviews, he was loving every second of it. In the meantime, Harbor Regional Hospital had cautiously given permission for her to donate her kidney to Robby. There would be more forms and doctors involved than normal, but they would go forward as soon as the transplant team completed more tests on her and Robby. Robby might not have changed much, but she could almost care about him from a distance. Her parents had yet to try and contact her.

Nik nodded. "I'll let Catherine know."

Dani sank deeper into the couch. "You still haven't answered my question."

Nik couldn't meet her eyes, his tone sounded more resigned than questioning. "Can I love you and Dodger."

"No!" Dani sat up straight. Damn it. Men could be so thick sometimes. "Not Dodger. There is no Dodger. He's gone. Banished. Non-existent. I'm not even asking you to love Daniel. All I need to know is, can you be Daniel's friend?"

"His friend." Nik pulled back, thinking over her words.

"Yes. His friend." How could she make it any clearer? "Look. Daniel is a part of me. I can't pretend he doesn't exist. Not like I can with Dodger. I like being Daniel sometimes. I like to go to the gym and work out as Daniel. Or, go to the movies as Daniel. Or even, go dancing as Daniel. I'm not asking you to have sex with him. But I need to know, if I shift to Daniel every once in a while, can you walk down the street next to him as you would any other man? Like Thomas? Or, your father? Can you have a conversation with him over dinner?"

Nik didn't answer right away. Her words sparked his imagination. He too wondered if he could walk down the street with Daniel and reconcile the male side of her with Daniella, the woman who loved him. "Daniel and I did work together pretty well going after Fagin."

Dani's stomach relaxed around the ice cream. He was trying to understand. It wouldn't matter what size Dani shifted to in the future, Dodger was as dead as Fagin. There was still one detail she had to tell him. "Yes. I daresay you two made a pretty good team. The thing is, Nik — sometimes, when I sleep, I shift." She immediately raised a finger to his lips. "I know, I know, I'll have to tell the Oversight Committee about that, too. All I want to know, right now, is — if I shift during the night, can you deal with that?"

Nik blinked. "You mean sleep as in. . . ."

"Dreamy time sleepy land. Not sex. I already told you — no sex with Daniel."

"Has this been a problem in the past?"

Jerk. Making her talk about past relationships. Nik deserved the truth. "I have an ex-fiancé. He swore it would be okay until it actually happened. Then, he freaked. He was one of the main reasons, aside from the Alt ban, why I had to leave Star Haven."

"Your ex-fiancé was a foolish man," Nik said. "I'll do my best not to freak."

"Good." Dani's worry melted away to nothing. "All you really have to do is nudge me with your elbow and I'll shift back. It's not hard and doesn't take long. I promise. Besides, unexpected shifting is why I always sleep naked."

Nik's fingers found their way to her hair again, wrapping themselves around her curls. He had a familiar look in his eyes. Vain and wicked banished all thoughts of obeying the no skin-on-skin contact rule. Did Nik remember? Did he care? Nik had obeyed rules all of his life. Maybe this one time he didn't care, either. "You're staring, Nik. What are you thinking?"

"I'm thinking about how cute you look in those pajamas."

She grinned. For the first time in days, she wanted to smile and never stop. "Why, Nik, don't you know that I look even cuter out of my pajamas than I do in them?"

"Really?" he asked, his eyebrows raised, acting shocked.

"Yes, really. Do you want to take them off?"

"I do," he said. "But, first, I want you to go upstairs and pack up an overnight bag."

She frowned. "What do I need an overnight bag for?"

Nik leaned closer. "I'm taking you to my bed and this time I want you to stay there all night."

"Ooooo." She giggled. "All night in your big bed. What will I do with myself?"

He kissed her then. Kissed her like she'd never been kissed before. The kiss was unique, not because it was long, sensuous, and demanding, but because he gave her his heart. She could feel it beating against her hand as she worked the buttons on his shirt, one by one.

She wouldn't need that overnight bag tonight. She wasn't going to let Nik go for a long, long time.

ACKNOWLEDGEMENTS

Sometimes an author sits down to write a book. Other times the book sits the author down and tells them the story. *A Secret Rose* wasn't the story I was supposed to write this year, but Dani refused to let me write anything else. I surrendered to her charm and strong will.

Of course Dani wouldn't have a voice at all if it weren't for a few other people: Debra Doyle, Jan Jackson, Carla Mueller, Abigail Sharpe, Sheri Edmondson, and Jaye Garland. Thank you for helping me shape A Secret Rose into the story it has become.

OTHER STORIES FROM THUNDER CITY

VALLEY OF THE BLIND
A THUNDER CITY SHORT STORY

Below the surface, wishes become nightmares.
Seeker's extraordinary vision allows him to see the world layer by layer. When he peels back the layers of his own family however, he discovers secrets he wished he'd never learned. Soon after, he's kidnapped by terrorists hell-bent on starting a war with Thunder City. They plan to use Seeker as the catalyst, the fall guy for a political assassination. Can Seeker use his vision to save Thunder City and himself before it's too late?

SLOW BURN
A THUNDER CITY SHORT STORY

The vendetta of a lifetime will burn hotter if you mix it with water.
Spritz made headlines as child when the Happy Hooligan lured her into the woods on Halloween and terrorized her all night long. As an adult with the power to manipulate water, she's become a formidable

alternative human in her own right. When the Happy Hooligan returns to set the famous Thunder City boardwalk on fire, Spritz knows deep in her soul that his plans are more nefarious than watching the boardwalk burn. Stopping him will mean disobeying orders and could cost her the life she's worked so hard to rebuild.

STILL LIFE
A THUNDER CITY SHORT STORY

When angels guide your hand, failure is not an option.

Angels appear in Claire's artwork, warning her of tragedies before they occur. Despite society's belief that she's crazy, Claire can't turn her back on people who are in danger. When her angels warn her of a mass shooting about to happen, Claire risks her life to stop it, but will she have to give up her freedom forever to succeed?

BLOOD SURFER
A THUNDER CITY NOVEL, BOOK 1

Their destiny is written in blood.

Welcome to Star Haven, where the police arrest and imprison alternative humans, if not execute them outright. When outlaw Hannah Quinn saves Officer Scott Grey's life by bloodsurfing through his broken body, he winds up on the wrong side of the kill line.

Hannah blew any chance she had of escaping Star Haven when she chose to save Scott's life. Scott has a reputation for killing Alts instead of arresting them. Now that she's triggered his dormant Alt ability, he's forced to go on the run with her until she can break his despised Alt power.

Suspicion dies hard after a lifetime of conditioning. Despite the threat to their lives, Hannah finds herself falling for the one man she can't trust—and Scott falls for the woman who destroyed his life.

With love and mistrust at war in a city where betrayal can earn your freedom, will Hannah and Scott's tenuous bond be enough to save them?

AUTHOR BIO:

A Connecticut Yankee transplanted to Central Florida, Debra Jess writes science fiction, romance, urban fantasy, and superheroes. She began writing in 2006, combining her love of fairy tales and Star Wars to craft original stories of ordinary people in extraordinary adventures and fantastical creatures in out-of-this world escapades. Her first published novel, *Blood Surfer*, has won the National Excellence in Romance Fiction Award for Best Paranormal and Futuristic.

Debra is a graduate of Viable Paradise and is a member of Codex. She›s also a member of the Romance Writers of America and RWA›s Fantasy, Futuristic, & Paranormal chapter and the First Coast Romance Writers.

You can sign-up for Debra Jess's newsletter on her website at **http://debrajess.com.**

You can also find her on social media at:
Bookbub | Facebook | Twitter | Pinterest | Tumblr | Instagram

Made in the USA
Columbia, SC
28 June 2017